FINDING TIGER

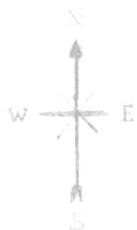

Also by Gabriel Schirm

Sunrises to Santiago

FINDING TIGER

A Novel

Gabriel Schirm

PAZ
~ PUBLISHING ~

Finding Tiger. Copyright © 2017 by Gabriel Schirm. All rights reserved. Published in the United States by Paz Publishing LLC, Denver. No part of this publication may be reproduced or transmitted in any form or by any means, mechanical or electronic, including photocopying and recording, or by any information storage and retrieval system, without permission in writing from the author or publisher (except by a reviewer, who may quote brief passages and/or show brief video clips in a review). For information, address Paz Publishing LLC, PO Box 9041, Denver, CO 80209.

Paz Publishing LLC Paperback Published 2017.

Library of Congress Control Number: 2017908539

ISBN 978-0-9861224-4-6 paperback

Printed in the United States of America

For Amy, my coffee shop girl, and to Gramps

Compass
(noun): a device that is used to find direction by means of a needle that always points north.

(verb): to devise or contrive often with craft or skill.

CHAPTER ONE

I have no internal compass. I'm almost certain of that. You know those people who know exactly where they are headed in life and then giggle and happily skip until they get there? That's not me. I'm 33 years old, and I still don't have a clue where I'm going, much less how I'm going to get there. Those people with actual goals and life maps are alien to me. Good for them I guess, but I still can't help but hate them.

I want happiness just like the people who plan ahead. I want love for example. Not the sex kind. Well actually that kind of love is great, too. But I want real love. I ache for it, which I admit is an odd thing for a grown man to say. I want the kind of love that I saw in my parents. I also want my parents. I want to change the awful thing that happened to them. I wish I could change myself and turn back time. The problem is that everything I want seems to be hidden inside of an impenetrable fog or even worse, lost forever.

I have even managed to misplace the most important green plastic compass in the world. This is as ironic as it is true. The fact that I can't find it bothers me a lot. It belonged to my parents. It reminds me of a time when I felt like life made sense. Gramps is going to kill me if he finds out that I lost it.

I live in downtown Denver, but I spend a weekend every month visiting my Gramps up near Gunnison. Most people call him Charles, or sometimes Chuck, but Gramps was the name I gave him when I spoke my first words and it stuck. He lives by himself in a modest cabin, with two floors and a cellar, which smells of wet dirt and motor oil but even so, I feel safe down there, among the spiders and crickets.

The cellar is directly under the cabin and two large green doors covered with peeling paint open from the cellar to the dirt driveway out front. Gramps stores his tired red Toro lawn mower down there, along with mounds of old things like paint cans, big blue tarps, boxes of nails, screws, matches and mousetraps that are always somehow covered in mouse droppings.

Sometimes I get nostalgic and go through all of the lawn games in the cellar. I don't really ever know what I am looking for, and I never seem to find it. I always leave feeling depressed. Dust-covered games line the time-worn wooden shelves. Games like horseshoes, badminton, and the large tin can we used to use to play *kick the can* with when Mom was still alive. Mom used to yell, "Olly, olly, oxen, free," into the night, and I would sprint back to the cabin through the midsummer mountain air. God, how I loved that game.

I could close my eyes anywhere in the world and see the cabin in my mind. I know it like I know my own face. The fireplace is my favorite part of the cabin and where Gramps and I spend most of our time, enjoying fires in the evenings, sitting in the two big comfy leather armchairs that face the fire. We try not to talk about my parents, especially after the sun goes down. It just hurts too much. Everything in the cabin is made of wood, which— combined with the pine furniture, the walls, and the floor— makes you feel as if you are living inside of one big tree.

There is a nest of chicken wires on top of the large stone chimney that sticks out of the north side of the cabin. I had to cover the opening of the chimney last summer because woodchucks kept getting inside and waking Gramps up in the middle of the night. He bolted out of bed one early morning to the loud chirp of a woodchuck in his ear. He fled into the pitch-dark living room, and hit his head on a wall he forgot was there. It knocked him out cold, so we decided, for safety's sake, that I better do something about the problem.

Two large lilac bushes frame the outside of the cabin, which are Grammy's doing. I love to look at them in the predawn light when Gramps and I usually head out to go fishing. In the early morning the purple flowers are dark indigo. She planted them years ago.

There is a grove of aspen trees on the hill above the cabin, where deer and elk like to hang out. Once a curious black bear came down from the trees and scared Grammy half to death. I watched her running, which I had never seen her do, across the sage-filled meadow in front of the cabin. She was screaming and yelling at Gramps, who was fidgeting with his lawn mower. I spotted what they were hollering about, meandering down from the aspen grove.

The large black bear looked almost friendly as it made its way down towards us. Grammy and Gramps got inside and locked all the doors. Gramps grabbed the shotgun from the cellar and we waited to be killed. The bear was harmless, though. It sniffed around the cabin for about half an hour, grabbed a drink from the stream, and then made its way slowly back up into the aspen grove. Grammy didn't let me play outside for months after that.

The cabin is smack dab in the middle of an old ghost town called Baldwin. Most people have never heard of it. There are nine crumbling cabins left over from this coal mining town's heyday back in the early 1900s. Our cabin is the 10th. Gramps says about 200 people used to live in Baldwin. There even used to be a post office, hotel, saloon, and a company store along with the 40 or so log homes scattered around the valley. Most of them are now just big mounds of dirt and decomposing logs.

Gramps, Grammy, Mom, Dad and I would explore the old one-room cabins looking for hidden treasures when I was a kid. We would find tattered newspapers, leather shoes, glass jars, Coke bottles, bedsprings, doll heads, toy cars, tin cans, and even cast iron stoves. My favorite building is the broken-down school house. Antique desks and a big green chalkboard remain inside as if the people who lived and went to school there left in a hurry. The post office closed in 1949 and with that, people just disappeared.

Down a small hill below the schoolhouse is the forgotten mineshaft. Iron tracks, now covered with grass and blooming wildflowers, lead into a dark hole in the ground. Today, there is a tired wire fence set up in a circle around the mine shaft with a sign that says, *DANGER! DO NOT ENTER.* I never have had the courage to explore the mine, even though it is incredibly tempting. It was especially so when I was a boy.

Gramps and I don't explore the cabins that surround ours much anymore. We don't play lawn games either. We fish and talk about everything. Gramps is my best friend, and my guess is that he would say the same about me.

I can't wait to tell him about the girl I just met. Her name is Isabel. Isabel from Spain. I haven't been this excited about anything really, in a long long time. Love at first sight is stupid, or at least it is until something like this happens to you. It's like ghosts. What I mean is, I won't believe in ghosts until I actually see one. Until that day all the "ghost believers" of the world are morons in my book.

Now I am the moron. She walked into the coffee shop, and I finally understood what all those starry-eyed love birds in the movies are always gushing about. It was inexplicable. It was magic, and I don't even believe in magic anymore. Before she spoke a word to me, she made me forget that Grammy and my parents are gone. She made me forget that I work at Speedy Coffee for a living and don't have the balls to open my own shop.

The small problem, or what one might call a roadblock, is that I can't seem to find the napkin she left on the counter. The one with her phone number on it.

In a single week I have managed to lose my parents' old compass and the only means of contacting the possible love of my life. Maybe Gramps will know what to do.

CHAPTER TWO

This will be our 20th summer fishing together; fishing what Gramps calls the most beautiful river in the world. I remember the first fish I caught up here, a small rainbow trout that glistened and sparkled like a colorful diamond I had plucked from the gray water. My nine-year-old self thought it to be a whale, wriggling at the end of my line. I imagined it could pull me into the river, never to be seen again.

"Fish on!" Gramps yelled so loud at the site of that catch that the mourning doves, blackbirds, and finches exploded out of the trees in the valley.

His reaction filled me with adrenaline as he let me struggle to reel in my fish. I remember the exciting feeling of something alive and strong tugging at the end of my line. It darted around, zigzagging under the water, before jumping above the surface, trying to free itself from my hook, which thrilled me to the core. When I finally held it in my hands, I stared at the fish, which was struggling to breathe. I froze. Never had I held a life in my hands.

"Do you want to eat it or let it live?" Gramps had asked.

I wanted the fish to live. Something inside of me did not want to kill.

"Eat it," I blurted out without knowing why. I must have

thought that it was what Gramps wanted to hear.

"Then we have to kill it and end its suffering," he said.

He grabbed the fish, removed the hook, and smashed its head on a large rock next to the river. After I heard the thick thud of rock against flesh, the trout went limp. Gramps quickly fed a string through one gill and out of its mouth and then placed the fish in a small pool of water on the side of the river. I watched in horror as blood slowly left the fish's head and formed a trickle of red water as it joined the clear river.

I hid my face with my small white fishing hat and cried. I fought with all of my body, but the tears came fast. I felt a hand on my shoulder. I was ashamed.

"It's OK, Tiger," he said. "This is the beauty of life. I know it's hard, but Grammy won't waste that fish. You have a big heart, boy. God knows we need more people like you in this world."

I cried every time I killed a fish that summer, but eventually it got easier. Gramps bought me my very own Swiss Army knife and taught me how to clean the fish before we brought them back to the cabin for Grammy. Ironically, now I can kill a fish without emotion, but we don't kill many of them anymore since Grammy isn't here to cook them for us.

"Tiger!" Gramps yells from downstairs. Louder than the first time. "Time to get up!" He taps the ceiling with something, possibly the handle of a broom.

"What time is it?" I ask. My voice cracks as I look around the cold, dark room. I stretch my arms above my head, releasing the cobwebs that seem to be caught in my body. Taking a deep breath, I yawn and rub my tired eyes.

"Four thirty. C'mon. Get up or the fish will be full by the time we get to the river," Gramps says as he makes his way up the creaky wooden stairs. The faint glow from the kitchen downstairs lights his way. He flips on the bedside lamp, and the yellow light illuminates his face, wrinkled and full of boyish excitement. The gray stubble of his unshaven face darkens in the crevices of his deep wrinkles. Gramps loves fishing and so do I.

"OK, OK," I mumble as I roll out of bed.

I brush my teeth, throw on my clothes, and pull up my waders. It is a crisp September morning, and the smell of freshly brewed coffee fills the air. I breathe in deep, and the aroma causes a smile to break out across my face. It mixes with the musty air of this old cabin and the fresh air of the pine and aspen trees that surround us. The smell is as real as any memory, and of summers now long gone.

Gramps moves slower than he used to. Every year he seems to hunch forward a little more. His hair is now a mix of gray and white, and his belly looks like he stole it from Santa Claus.

This morning Gramps is wearing a long sleeve red and black checkered flannel shirt, white sneakers, and black suspenders to keep his loose blue jeans in place. The left breast pocket of his shirt holds fishing pliers and fingernail clippers to cut fishing line. The right breast pocket carries his white handkerchief, which he is never without. He takes a big sip of coffee from the coffee mug I gave him years ago for Christmas. It says, *World's Best Grandad*.

He watches me, impatiently, as I come down the stairs. He already has on his baby blue fishing hat and wide clear-rimmed glasses.

"Are you ready yet?" he asks and looks down at my waders. "Oh no. I can't be seen with you. Really I can't. You look like a real square. Waders? Really? Eat this."

He grabs a granola bar from a giant box he must have picked up at Costco and throws it to me.

"Ha, ha," I sarcastically reply. "Let's go."

We head out the door of the cabin and hop into Gramps's beat up old green pickup truck. The door creaks and groans as I pry it open.

"You aren't going to cry today are ya, Tiger?" Gramps says

with a smile as we pull out of the dirt driveway.

"That gets funnier every year," I reply.

The headlights illuminate the path through the morning darkness. Gramps hands me a silver thermos filled with hot coffee.

"Thanks," I say. "What kind?"

Gramps looks over at me as he steers the rusty truck over a poorly maintained dirt road. He takes a big bite of a granola bar and stares at me. The truck lurches off the road, running over a few sage bushes, before he releases his gaze and corrects the truck.

"It's coffee. The kind of coffee real people drink. Country people. People that don't wear waders. I can't afford your fancy, sustainably raised, powder puff traded, two bean roasted, came out of a monkey's buttock, rainbow farm shit," he says.

"You are insulting my profession."

"You work at Speedy Coffee, Tiger."

"For now. For now," I say and take a big gulp of hot coffee. It is good enough.

Gramps and I navigate slowly through Baldwin, Colorado, the ghost town that our cabin used to be a part of, and pass Joe Peanut's grave. The truck's headlights illuminate old logs, crumbling around broken-down doorframes as we follow the narrow dirt road.

"Who was Joe Peanut again?" I ask Gramps as we round the bend and drive onto the main dirt road that connects us with the outside world. We approach an intersection. There, a green sign with two arrows—one pointing left to Gunnison and the other pointing right towards Crested Butte—stands crooked on the side of the road. We turn right and continue our journey down Ohio Creek Road.

"He was an old fella I met when I was a kid. He was friends with my dad, your great gramps. He was the last miner left here in Baldwin. When he died, well, our cabin was the last one left with any human inhabitants. Now it's just me up here. Me and the woodchucks," he says.

"Why did they call him Joe Peanut?"

"Well he was always sittin' on his front porch over there," he says pointing to a dilapidated cabin that no longer has a roof. Large wild rose bushes growing from the inside push out of the glassless windows. I can still make out what must have been a small front porch.

"He would sit there, crunching on peanuts all day, from dawn till dusk, without fail. He had a big yellow rocking chair, which he would sit on, rocking back and forth, eating peanuts. There was always a giant pile of peanut shells next to him. I swear the pile was as tall as he was sitting there," he recalls with a look in his eye that tells me he can still see the shells and smell the peanuts. "So we called him Joe Peanut. And he answered to it, too. My dad used to yell to him when we were headed to the river to fish, 'Heya, Joe Peanut.' And I would repeat, 'Heya, Joe Peanut.' And Joe would just wave, crack another peanut and rock back and forth."

The imagined scene plays clearly in my mind, because Joe Peanut's cabin is an exact replica of ours, just like all of the crumbling cabins in this valley.

"I wish you would move into town. I don't like you spending all of your time alone up here," I say.

Gramps pulls the truck over to the side of the road and parks it in a thicket of tall grass and mud next to a black sign with bright orange letters that reads, *No trespassing. Private property. Keep out.*

"Baldwin is my home, Tiger. I can't afford to live in town anyway," he says. This is an argument we have had a hundred times. "Besides, you know me, it's not that I don't like people, it's just that I haven't met many people that I like."

We grab our fishing poles and tackle boxes before bending down to pass through a gap in the barbed wire fence. I cross first and carefully lift the top wire while pushing the bottom down with my foot to make it easier for Gramps to maneuver his way through. We make our way down towards Ohio Creek, aiming for a grove of cottonwood trees that Gramps and I have been fishing for years.

Seeing the *No Trespassing* signs again makes me uneasy. This used to be open space when I was younger. That is until a man bought the land a few years back and put up all of those *No Trespassing* signs along with miles and miles of new barbed wire fences. This is a man Gramps calls "a real son of a bitch." We have been chased off this land more times than I can count, but we keep coming back. Gramps considers it a God-given right since our family has been fishing here for two centuries.

"Think he will see us today?" I ask Gramps as we walk through a pasture filled with dew-covered grass and clover. The grass is waist high, and I am thankful for my city boy waders that are keeping my legs dry.

"Nah. That bastard is scared of me," he says, looking over at me with a mischievous twinkle in his eye.

I take a deep breath of the crisp cool morning air. My exhale is visible in the cold. The mountains that surround us seem to breathe as well, as they stand tall like watchmen over the valley below.

The sun peeks over the mountains and shines on the green-gold blades of tall grass and sage bushes. I reach down to grab a handful of sage, pausing to rub it between my hands and inhale the powerful aroma. The dew drops that cling to the grass and intricate spider webs look like tiny diamonds.

I step in a giant wet cow patty, a gift from Jim. He has almost 300 head of cattle roaming around on his land, making it nearly impossible not to step in cow pies now and again. We amble into the grove of cottonwoods, and I hear the calming sound of the river before I can see it.

"So tell me about this girl," Gramps says as he sets his fishing pole next to the river. He takes a moment to adjust his suspenders. His jeans are soaked from the walk through the grass.

"You are going to think I'm crazy," I say.

"What's new?" he says. "C'mon Tiger, you and I are lonely losers. Tell this old man about the dame."

We prepare our fly rods by unwinding the line and untangling the knots that seem to have magically formed during our short journey from the cabin. I select my spot, a small bend in the river where the fast-moving water slows into a deep calm pool, and I can practically see the rainbow trout lurking in the dark water. I squint into the sun and grab my sunglasses from the front pocket of my waders. Mosquitos and blackflies are easily visible in the sunlight, hovering above the slower pools of Ohio Creek.

I grab a small glass jar from my tackle box and swipe it into a thick cloud of bugs, quickly closing the top so they can't escape. I hold up the captured bugs to the light, examining their tiny legs, wings, and bodies. I compare them to my flies and select a fuzzy looking, brown Elk Hair Caddis.

"You gonna tell me about this girl or not?" he asks again.

"OK, OK. Well, I met her last week. She came into the coffee shop and I made her an espresso," I say.

"What's her name?" Gramps asks as he skillfully lands his fly on a calm pool near some willows next to the river. His old white tennis shoes are submerged in ice-cold river water.

"Isabel." I can't help but smile.

"Well, are you going to call her?" Gramps asks. "You are old as hell so you better hurry it up before you're dead. You're gonna be 40 before you know it." He looks suspicious and amused.

"Well, that's the thing. She gave me her number. She wrote it on a napkin. I swear I put the napkin in my pocket, but I lost it," I reply.

"You are one unlucky fella," Gramps says as he laughs and lifts his rod and casts his fly again, landing it on top of the slow-moving water. I watch it drift downstream for a second or two as he continues his interrogation. "What do you remember about her?"

"I know this is going to sound stupid, but I have never felt that feeling. That thing. I was mesmerized by her," I try to explain. "I can't stop thinking about her. It was like time sort of stopped or something when I first saw her. It's driving me crazy."

"Can't you get on your internet and find her on the Google?" he asks.

"I wouldn't know what to look for. All I know about her is that she is from Spain and on vacation. A solo trip. Isabel is beautiful. *Really* beautiful. She has big brown eyes and smiled with them. She seems to have a big heart and plays the guitar. Her love of coffee is awesome, and I don't know, when I saw her it was like a bolt of lightning hit me in the chest. I can't describe it. I couldn't stop staring at her. She probably thought I was a crazy person, but she laughed at my jokes. Oh and her Spanish accent, wow, I could listen to that all day. I mean all day, Gramps."

"What did you talk about that was so amazing?"

"I don't know really. It's funny, I mostly remember the *feeling* of talking to her. Let's see. Well, she asked me about my tattoos. She told me she loved whipped cream with coffee, and I promised to forgive her for that. She loves wildflower honey and bees. Oh and I told her about Mom and Dad's compass because I was holding it while we were chatting. I think she was about to cry, so I stopped telling her the story. You know. Then she put her hand on mine, and I almost died."

"Is that how you pick up girls? Tell them that your parents are dead?" Gramps asks and shakes his head.

"Hey, I didn't bring it up. Anyway, then she asked me to call her Isa. We ended up talking for only about half an hour. She gave me her number then left."

"Eeeesa?" Gramps repeats my pronunciation.

"She was like, it's hard to describe, like pure good. I felt like she was a friend I had always had but somehow we just met. It sounds nuts, I know." I cast my line in the 10-o'clock, 2-o'clock position, again and again, just like Gramps taught me when I was younger. I ask Gramps for some genuine advice. "What should I do?"

He doesn't reply so I take my eyes off my line to glance his way. I see pain in his face. "Grow a pair will ya. You always do this. You have to find her. Now shut up and stop scaring all the fish," he says. His voice cracks with emotion as he retrieves his white handkerchief from his pocket and wipes his eyes.

He is probably thinking about Grammy or maybe even Mom, so I leave him alone. We fish in silence. The river is beautiful today as it always is. The cottonwood leaves are turning yellow, signs that fall is here and winter will soon follow. I watch a water spider make its way around my feet submerged in the clear river water.

I know Gramps is right, although I feel ridiculous. I need to find her but I no longer believe in impossible things, in love. That belief in the magic of life died when my parents disappeared. I am a realist now and no matter how badly I want it, I know all good things will eventually end. I have always been unlucky in this area. Always the dumped. Always the fool. Maybe if Mom was still around I would know what to say to women.

Somehow I need to find Isabel. This person from Spain whose number I have managed to lose has captured my imagination. "I'm an idiot," I mutter, my voice drowned out by the river. I will turn 34 soon enough and probably have to endure a lifetime of other people's baby showers, weddings, and dinner plans where quirky Uncle Atlas is always the third wheel.

"Judas Priest," Gramps yells as he quickly makes his way to a large clump of willows next to the shore where he proceeds to sit in the middle of the foliage.

"What are you doing?" I yell. "You are gonna get ticks all over you."

"Shhh. I see the Texan coming. Hide," he whispers loudly.

I follow his eyes and spot Jim, who is wearing a brown cowboy hat, matching boots, and a green flannel shirt tucked into soiled blue jeans, marching through the field over the opposite bank of the river. He takes big steps over the tall grass, his loaded rifle aimed at the ground. I am not sure what makes me more nervous—the rifle or his snarling dog.

"Get up. He already sees us," I whisper back to Gramps. "You are going to break your hip, get up."

I cast my fishing line in defiance as Jim slowly approaches our location. A redneck if I have ever seen one. Gramps hates him even more because he is from Texas. According to Gramps, Texans are taking over Colorado.

Jim, the owner of this land, looks to be my age, maybe in his early to mid 30s. He has a giant black mustache, and his left cheek is full of tobacco.

"Well, good morning, Atlas. Charles. Looks like you don't ever learn. This is private property. I am going to have to ask y'all to leave," Jim struggles to project calm, but anger bubbles beneath the surface of his voice. His thick Texan accent extends each word.

"Screw you, Jim. You know we have been fishing here longer than you have even lived in Colorado," I reply. His face flushes red, and he bites his lower lip.

"I don't give a flying fart if your grandpappy's, daddy's daddy fished here. We don't call the police round here," he says as he pats his rifle. I have been hearing stories of these "damn Texans" my entire life. He has yet to shoot at us but every time he threatens us with his gun, it makes me uneasy.

He spits a line of dark tobacco on the ground and pauses before looking back in our direction and wiping dark spit from his chin.

"Nice mustache, Texas," Gramps yells, shaking the branches of his bush. He hasn't moved.

"Gramps, shut up. I got this," I whisper back.

"You aren't going to shoot an old man and his grandson. We aren't hurting anybody, and we haven't even caught any fish," I say, trying to reason with Jim. I feel my hand shaking as it tries to hold my fly rod steady. He doesn't reply and spits again. His dog, a giant German Shepherd, won't stop barking. The muscular beast is prowling the bank of the river, looking for a way to cross and tear into us both.

I cast my line again. I am trying to act tough and indifferent, but the truth is I hate confrontation.

"Your face looks like a dime's worth of dog meat," Gramps yells from his bush.

"What? Gramps, shut up. What does that even mean?" I whisper back.

"I am only going to ask one more time nicely," Jim retorts. "You both need to leave immediately."

I look him in the eyes and cast my line again in defiance. All of a sudden, a gunshot explodes through the air and causes me to fall into the water. The sound echoes off the mountains around us. I drop my pole and check myself for blood. My ears are ringing.

"Gramps are you OK?" I yell.

"I'm fine. He just shot into the air. You are not gonna die," he replies.

"You are crazy, Jim!" My face is warm with anger.

"I told y'all to leave." He is laughing at me, but his voice is still full of rage. I watch Jim's face turn from anger to confusion as his jaw drops. He is looking behind me in the direction of the willows. I follow his gaze.

Gramps has dropped his pants and is mooning Jim in all of his bare bottomed, old man glory.

We both look on, perplexed. A flood of curse words tumbles from Jim's mouth as he starts to cross the river, wading into the water directly across from where I am standing. The dog tries to follow, whimpering, trying to find a dry path.

I grab my fishing pole and help Gramps pull up his pants as we quickly gather our belongings and head towards the truck in the opposite direction. I glance back over my shoulder. Jim is headed our way, fast.

Gramps won't stop laughing.

"Shut up, Gramps! This is serious. Jesus," I shout as we slowly make our escape. A 75-year-old man can't exactly move quickly.

Another gunshot blasts through the air echoing off the mountains, and Gramps instinctively covers his head. We continue, finally making it to the barbed wire fence, quickly crossing back through to safety. Fresh bullet holes greet us at the truck, smoking from side of the door.

"What the hell, Jim," I yell back weakly.

We climb into the cab of the truck, and I start the engine as quickly as I can. Jim seems satisfied and is slowly retreating towards the river. The dog never crossed, thankfully.

I glare at Gramps who can't seem to catch his breath. Tears of joy drip from his eyes and gather on the gray stubble covering his cheeks like the dew on the grass outside.

"I think ... I think ... ," he gasps for air between fits of laughter. "I think I have peed my pants."

"I don't doubt it, you old geezer."

He laughs all the way to the cabin. I squeeze the steering wheel until my knuckles turn white and vow revenge that I know will never come.

CHAPTER THREE

I was born in a VW van to travelers. My parents were in the middle of a long multi-state road trip, camping, exploring, and adventuring when I decided to enter this world. I came a few weeks early. It was their honeymoon, and they were taking some time to drive from Fresno, California, to Denver, Colorado.

It was the eighties, but when I look at the photos from that trip, my parents looked like they had never left the sixties. My mom used to say that babies are greatly affected by the "vibes" that surround the mother, and she always used to tell me I was one of the lucky few who had pretty amazing "vibes" while I was growing in her womb.

They called their love "magic." They used this word often, and I can see it in their photos now. I am sad to say, I am forgetting details about them, but I guess that is why people take photographs. The photos are stored in a three-ring photo binder that I keep at the cabin. I have had to start limiting the amount of times I allow myself to take the photos out of their protective plastic sheets. I like to hold them in my hands. It makes my parents feel closer somehow, but over the years the pictures have started to show signs of fading from my oily fingerprints. I feel terrible because a particular favorite of mine is now almost unrecognizable. I have touched their faces so many times that the details of the photograph have faded completely. Only white orbs remain.

There is one treasured photo in particular that was taken on the side of the road in Zion National Park in Utah. This Polaroid was taken about two days before I was born. Their green and white Volkswagen van is only half visible in the left side of the photo. *Wash Me* is written in the dust on the back window. The words are enclosed in a giant heart, and there is a peace symbol drawn next to that, most likely by Dad.

My parents are posed in the middle of the picture with a spectacular view behind them of giant mountains made of red-stoned rocks. The sun is setting and the tips of the tops of the rocks seem to be glowing orange red as the last rays of the day's sun illuminates their craggy faces.

Mom is resting her head on Dad's shoulder as they face the camera. They are both smiling. The smiles are genuine and real. Dad's long dark brown beard is wild, and he is wearing aviator sunglasses. He has on ripped jean shorts, a big white-collar shirt that is unbuttoned, and a tie-dyed bandanna wrapped around his head.

A crown of white flowers sits atop Mom's braided hair. The sun shines brightly, and she squints as a few strands of loose brown hair blow across her face. Her white sundress flutters in the same direction as her hair, towards the van. Dad's right hand rests on her stomach. His left hand is holding a slice of cantaloupe, which is dripping all over the ground. I am the size of a watermelon in Mom's womb.

I can see that "magic" they spoke of in the photo. The way they are touching each other speaks of a carefree love. Their eyes are filled with joy, and the good "vibes" that must have surrounded us all that day.

I was born in a campsite deep in the heart of Zion National Park. We were surrounded not by humans, but by woods full of mule deer, bighorn sheep, mountain lions, and great horned owls hidden in the piñon pine and cottonwood trees. Plants like claret cup cactus, butterfly weed, Zion shooting star flowers, desert paintbrush, and old man sagebrush welcomed me into this world.

The fact that I was born this way and not in a hospital enraged my grandparents. They called it reckless. My parents called it natural and beautiful. My grandparents said there should have been doctors around, and my parents said I was brought into this world by moonbeams and starlight.

They used the torn-out pages of a large atlas to line the back of the van where I was born at 2:00 a.m. with no complications at all. Dad had read how to cut an umbilical cord, and they saved it for later. They dried part of it and put it in an envelope, to capture the good "vibes" of that day and save them forever. My parents named me Atlas to honor the occasion, and Mom liked the idea that the name would always help me find direction in this world.

"I am sorry, but we have to call off the search. We have exhausted all of our resources," the policeman said. This is the worst sentence I have ever heard to date.

I was only eight, but I remember certain things about that day as if they had happened only a few hours ago. I remember the policeman's mustard stain on his right shoulder. The feeling of cold plastic when he handed me the compass. The smell of aftershave. I stared at the black gun holstered in his belt and the walkie-talkie that would amplify a faraway voice relaying numbers of some kind. I especially remember the terror I felt when I heard Gramps howl with rage and misery. Grammy slowly and silently sobbed.

I had never seen Gramps or Grammy cry. I had never thought about it, but up until that point, I didn't know they could be sad, or could express negative emotions. I thought grandparents were immune to sorrow.

Gramps began to hurl insults at the policeman through his tears. To me it seemed like hours, but I am sure it only lasted for a few minutes. I hid in the closet and watched them argue through the spaces between my Mom's favorite dresses. The policeman looked incredibly uncomfortable as he tried to calm Gramps down and console Grammy. Inside the closet, I wrapped Mom's big purple scarf around my ears to block out the noise. I could still smell her lavender perfume as I buried my nose in the knit wool.

My parents were gone. It was now official, this much I understood. They told me as much as an eight-year-old boy should know, but I struggled to accept it.

They had gone for a hike and they never returned. Worst of all, it was my fault.

I had saved for months to buy them a wedding anniversary present. This was a date they both celebrated with gusto every year. They were madly in love. Their magic was still very much alive even eight years after that night in Zion National Park when I was born.

Gramps took me to the sporting goods store a week before Mom and Dad's big weekend, and I was overwhelmed by the selection. I knew I wanted to get them a compass but I didn't know which one.

To make money to buy the gift, I delivered newspapers during the early morning hours; I sold lemonade from our front yard and iced tea from the red wagon I wheeled around downtown Gunnison. I walked my neighbor's dogs, and I served as my grandparents' official map navigator whenever we would drive somewhere together. For this, Grammy would always give me five dollars upon safe arrival at our destination.

It had to be a compass. We would always visit Grammy and Gramps up at the cabin every Sunday. It was my favorite thing to do in the whole world. During the week, Gramps would always hide a purple plastic egg, with something exciting inside, a treasure, somewhere in Baldwin. Dad had gotten me a nice black metal compass for my seventh birthday, and he and Mom taught me how to use it by going on these treasure hunts.

Each week Gramps would prepare a short list of clues for me to follow, using my compass. He would write things like

1.) *Head north when you get to the big pine tree next to Joe Peanut's grave.*
2.) *When you first see the mine shaft head west until you get to the schoolhouse.*
3.) *Head east five paces and dig under the front porch of the cabin with no roof.*

Inevitably, I would get confused and lost, fiddling with my compass and trying to figure out where the purple plastic egg was buried.

Dad would remind me that the fun of this was the search, not the finding of the egg. Mom would agree, kiss Dad on the cheek, and I would either calm down or throw a tantrum. Eventually we would find the egg and inside Gramps would have stored something just for me. Things like a new fly for fishing, chocolate, money, a miniature plastic magnifying glass, or even sometimes a new set of clues.

So, when it came time for me to get my parents a gift, I wanted it to be a compass of their own. At the sporting goods store, they were big, small, metal, gold, and plastic. They came in every color and price range you could think of. I still remember exactly what Gramps said to me as I stood there, staring at the massive wall of options.

"Choose wisely, Tiger. A compass can keep them safe in the woods. A compass will make sure they always find their way home."

I chose a small cheap army green plastic compass because I

wanted to use some of the extra money I had saved to buy chocolate for myself. The circular compass opened and closed like a pocket watch, and had a white and red needle balanced in the middle of bold white letters printed on a perfect black circle; *N, S, E* and *W*. Gramps asked me if I was sure. It was a selfish and childish choice.

Gramps and Grammy would always watch me every year while my parents went off on some trip or adventure for the weekend to celebrate their union. Their love made me gag when I was eight, but looking back on it now, they had a love that I desperately want someday. Maybe it was because that was a time in my life when I last felt happy, safe, and home. It was the last time I believed in magic.

That year my parents planned a weekend trip to go hike a 14,000-foot mountain, a *fourteener*, somewhere near Buena Vista, Colorado. I wrapped the compass in old newspaper comics and gave it to them as they were packing to leave.

Mom opened the gift, and when I told her it was to make sure she could always find her way, she cried. I was confused. I thought she hated it. Dad made me tell him how it worked, which I made up mostly, as he coaxed me along.

"This will always point north, so then you can go, um, well north," I remember saying. "You have to hold it like this."

To which Dad replied, "This is a fine gift, Atlas. We love it. Don't worry, we will use it all weekend so we don't get lost."

He ruffled my hair, and I escaped to my room to gorge on the two giant Hershey's chocolate bars under my pillow. The ones I bought with the extra money.

I watched them through the curtain from my bedroom window, completely satisfied with my chocolate, as they packed their rusty green and white Volkswagen van. They looked so happy and content. I was, too. Dad was wearing dark blue jeans and a gray wool sweater. Mom, a flower dress and brown Birkenstock sandals. She had flowers in her hair.

Dad carried out their navy blue tent, water jugs, cooler, backpacks, green canvas camping chairs, and beer. My grandparents pulled up to the front of the house in their white sedan, and I watched them talk with Mom as Dad slowly filled the van with gear and checked the engine oil.

Mom showed them the compass and I smiled, before shoving the second chocolate bar in my mouth and heading outside to see them off. It was the last time I ever saw them alive.

Gramps started paying me 20 dollars for my navigational duties after that. He also bought me all the chocolate I wanted and picked fights with the parents of kids who were mean to me at school. I remember years later, in high school, I told him one day that a kid at school had called me a bastard, because I didn't have any parents. I asked him what exactly the definition of a bastard was. He left without answering me, got in the car, and came back three hours later. Grammy asked him what happened to his knuckles, which were bleeding, and he just went to bed, without saying a word.

I have only recently read all of the newspaper articles about my parents' disappearance. Gramps wouldn't allow me to read anything or even watch the news after they vanished. I suppose he was trying to protect me in some way, and it wasn't too hard to shield me from the world living in the cabin. This couldn't dampen my curious obsession though.

About a year ago, when I finally mustered up the courage to read an article that was published about my parents in the Denver Post, I was overcome with emotion. The police found their campsite, but not my parents. When I saw the picture of their campsite, I couldn't breathe. The blue tent was erect, and their belongings were scattered everywhere, as if a bear had gone through their site, digging for scraps of food, and had flung sleeping bags, coolers and green canvas chairs everywhere. The cooler was undisturbed, which I found odd, as a bear surely would have dismantled it looking for dinner. The campsite was surrounded by thick woods. Blue spruce trees towered around their tent.

The thing that still haunts me is that the compass I gave them was in the black and white newspaper photo. It was sitting on a log, beside the rock campfire ring, next to Dad's old Swiss Army knife, his hiking boots and the flowers Mom had had in her hair the last time I saw them.

The compass top was flipped open. If only it could speak and tell the world what horrible things it witnessed. The reporter explained in the article that the evidence suggested foul play, but there was neither proof nor suspects. Those two things are missing to this day, and I suspect the police have all but forgotten about my parents. Their case file is likely stuffed in some dusty cardboard box along with all of the other forgotten souls.

The reporter who wrote the Denver Post article used words like *tragedy, disturbing, alarming* and *heartbreaking*. He referred to a little boy left behind. Their bodies were never found. Gramps never let me go camping again, and as I read the article I understood why.

I still blame myself for their deaths. This is something I have never told a soul. I feel like if I was a better person, I would have purchased a more expensive compass, and maybe, just maybe, they would have come home. It is irrational, I now know, but it made a lot of sense when I was young. I haven't been able to shake the guilt, which clings to me like my shadow. Besides, there is always the possibility that they just walked off into the woods and did actually become disoriented.

My parents' disappearance has killed my belief in magic and love, and without my parents I have always felt lost. I would give anything in the world to get them back. If only I could live up to the name that they gave me.

CHAPTER FOUR

"Double shot caramel macchiato," I call out to the crowd. It is busier than usual as I quickly prepare lattes, espressos, and frothy caffeinated beverages. I pause for a second to take a long delicious sip of my personal brew that I made at home. Just coffee, nothing else.

This particular blend comes from a small farm in Columbia that I had the opportunity to visit a few years ago on a backpacking trip through South America. I brought some beans home with me and gave them to a friend in town who runs a local roaster.

This is perfection in a cup. Citrus on the nose, earthy and delicious. I call them voodoo beans.

"Hey Atlas, c'mon," my stressed coworker Amanda shouts at me while steaming some milk. "Where is that double shot?"

I set down my voodoo drink and get to the task at hand, making mediocre coffee filled with more sugar than an entire chocolate cake. Someday I will have my own coffee shop. Someday. I wipe my hands on my green Speedy Coffee apron and get to work.

"How was your fishing trip?" Amanda asks.

"Gramps almost got us both shot, but good," I reply, then

shout out again to the crowd. "Double shot caramel macchiato. Dammit, where is this girl. Her coffee is getting cold."

"Oh hey, I almost forgot," Amanda says. "Remember that girl that came in last week? The Spanish girl you stared at like a serial killer rapist?" She bats her eyelashes, flips her blond curls behind her shoulder, and puckers her lips as if waiting for a kiss.

I roll my eyes and prepare another cup.

"You got her number, right? She left this here." She retrieves a guidebook stuffed behind the row of flavored syrups on the counter and holds it up for me to see. I lunge at the book and flip through its pages.

"Down boy," she replies. I don't pay any attention to her as I examine the cover of the book and its contents. My heart is racing. The title is written in big, bold, white letters on the cover: *Andalusia*. The picture on the cover is of a sparkling whitewashed hilltop Spanish village.

Why would a girl from Spain have a guidebook *for* Spain? I quickly flip through the book and see she has earmarked several pages and scribbled notes in the margins. She has written things like, *Si!, Bonita, Caro,* and *Tal vez?* inside. She has circled the names of some restaurants and underlined several cities in which she has also circled some neighborhoods.

"Hey. Dude, seriously," Amanda says taking my attention away from the book. "Look at this line. These people are going to murder us if we don't get them their coffee. Chop chop."

Amanda is over a decade younger than I am, but she is the manager of this store, which means she is my boss. I guess my lack of direction and motivation is the reason for this. She has grown on me though. She is a bright teenager with a good heart, and I couldn't dislike her if I tried. Still, it doesn't make it any easier to take orders from someone who gushes to me about her prom.

I get back to work and see the macchiato is still sitting on the counter getting cold. "Double shot caramel macchiato!" I try the crowd again. Finally, a teenager looks up from her phone and grabs the coffee.

"Excuse me. It's cold. Can you make me another?" she asks while simultaneously sending a text, never looking up from her phone. Amanda snickers. She knows this drives me crazy as I complain about people on their phones every morning. I realize I must sound like an old man to her. I think I have even used the phrase "kids these days" on several particularly frustrating mornings.

I swallow my pride and reply to the teenager, "Of course, right away." I hate this place. I took this job because I figured it would allow me to learn the coffee business before opening my own shop. I want to quit, but I need the money. I have rent and Gramps. Although he won't admit it, Gramps is running out of money himself. The cabin needs a new roof, and Gramps can't afford it. He also won't admit it because he is cheap. To him, any repair is simply an invention someone made up to take his money.

I dump a stale cup of espresso into a bowl, pop it into the microwave, return it to a new paper to-go cup and fill it half full with freshly steamed whole milk, then top it with several pumps of caramel and vanilla syrup. She won't be able to tell the difference between fresh coffee and old.

"Here ya go," I say, offering a giant fake smile and handing her the coffee. She doesn't look up from her phone, takes the drink, and leaves.

My shift passes quickly, as they do on particularly busy days, and it's finally time for me to head home. I can't wait to sit down in total, uninterrupted silence and examine every page of Isabel's guidebook. This desire makes me feel ridiculous. I have to remind myself that I don't believe in love at first sight, and I hate people who do. I imagine corny couples who dress alike and stroke each other's hair while they talk to you with starry eyes of contentment. But now look at me. I am obsessed with a girl who I met once and lives on another continent.

I hop on my brown fixed-gear bike, my only means of

transportation, and start pedaling home. A light gray drizzle begins to fill the autumn air as I head towards my studio apartment just outside of downtown Denver. I dart through traffic heading up 15th Street, into the Highlands neighborhood. The rain droplets feel refreshing on my cheeks, and I never grow tired of riding in the open air, no matter the time of year or the weather. My stomach groans. It is just about 2:00 p.m. and I haven't eaten lunch.

"Hey. Whaddya say, Atlas?" I hear a familiar voice as I pull off the street onto the sidewalk next to my apartment. He must have been sleeping under the metal stairs that lead up to my building.

"Hey, man. Here ya go, Gary," I hand him a steaming cup of coffee I brought from work.

"Yes, yes, yes," he rubs his hands together quickly to warm them up. "That's the stuff. That's the stuff."

Gary is the homeless guy who hangs out around my building. He loves coffee so I always try to remember to bring him some home from work. Oddly enough, I would even go so far as to call him my friend. I provide him with coffee, and he offers me someone to talk to, which is especially nice if I can catch him sober.

He has wild blond hair and piercing blue eyes. Most of the time Gary smells like a putrid mix of urine and booze, but he seems to me like someone who couldn't hurt a fly.

I take a seat on the steps beside him. He is sitting on a flattened cardboard box with his back up against the red brick wall. His elbow pokes through a hole in the Denver Broncos sweatshirt I gave him for Christmas last year.

"How was work?" he asks.

"Ahh, you know, work," I reply.

"I don't know," he says, laughing hard.

"I actually met a girl the other day, at work, and well, I really liked her. But I lost her information, so now I can't contact her," I say. Gary takes a big gulp of his coffee. Luckily, the direction of the breeze has changed, so I can't smell him anymore.

"I knew it. You were actually smilin' when you came home from work. I said to myself, that Atlas met a girl today, I just know it," he says. "You never smile. You always look sad."

"I do too smile," I reply.

"No you don't. It's about time you found a girl. You are a good lookin' guy. I thought you might be one of those gays though."

"One of *those gays*? Wow, Gary," I say. "You can't say stuff like that out loud."

"You deserve someone, really, nobody ain't ever been as nice to me as you have," he says, ignoring me.

"I don't know if I deserve someone, or believe that it's even possible anymore."

"Why not?" he asks.

"It's a long story. I'm selfish I guess, which ultimately led to the death of my parents. Not sure if I deserve much of anything," I mumble. I avoid eye contact with Gary and examine my hands, picking at my skin.

"Spare some change?" Gary says to a young couple walking past on the sidewalk. They hurry their pace and uncomfortably look at an imaginary object in the sky. Gary hasn't registered what I just said.

"How 'bout you, Gary? Ever think about getting a job, cleaning up, improving your lot in life?" I ask. He tears grass from the ground violently and tosses it on the sidewalk. I think I may have crossed some line.

"It ain't my fault I live down here. I used to have a family. I have a kid, you know. But my damn wife she ain't no use to nobody. She wouldn't let me have a damn beer. Not one damn beer when I came home from work. What the hell. How would you feel? You should have heard her naggin'. It woulda been enough to drive you away, too. I promise you," he yells and punches the ground with his fist.

"It's never just one, Gary. I will leave you, Gary. You can't be alone with our child, Gary," he says, imitating the voice of his wife in the ugliest way he possibly can, scrunching his lips and speaking in a high witchlike voice. "One day I came home and she had up and left. Not a note. Nothin'. I haven't seen or heard from 'em since. I never laid a hand on them or nothin'. I was just unreasonable to be around, or some shit. Damn princess, she pushed me here. And the homeless shelters and programs 'round here ain't good for nothin'. All these damn rules I gotta follow from do-good church folks. No sir, that ain't for me."

I don't know what to say. It's obvious he blames everyone but himself. He is unwilling to see his part in his story. He is as far from his true path as a man can get.

"You have got to see though, that you have at least some part in the circumstances of your life, right?" I timidly suggest. This might set him off, but I can't help it.

"I could say the same thing to you," he says flatly. He holds up his coffee in the air. "What should we cheers to? Hmm. To not deservin' love? To bein' lost? To whisky? Top o' the mornin' to ya!" he chuckles for a long time, a smoker's laugh, which ends in a coughing fit. When he calms down again, he lights up a cigarette.

"Enjoy your coffee, Gary," I say as I open up the door and carry my bike up the stairs to my apartment.

"You know I love you, Atlas," he calls after me.

"Yeah, yeah. Love you, too, Gary," I yell back.

I lock the door behind me, open the blinds and grab the guidebook from my bag. A pile of dirty clothes I left on the couch greets me. At least I *think* the clothes are dirty. I sniff at a shirt. Yep. Dirty. I swipe all of the clothes onto the floor and clear a space between the dirty dishes on the coffee table in the living room. The apartment is essentially a studio, but where the couch is situated, I call the living room. I look around my tiny apartment, at its tall ceiling, its old wooden floor, the tall dusty windows that look out on the neighboring brick building, and I can hear the words of Gramps in my head. He was not impressed when he saw this place.

"Wow. You are paying so much because the brick is exposed and crumbling? The pipes are showing, and you have homeless people for neighbors. This place is a dump," he told me upon is first inspection.

I head into the bathroom to take a shower, as I never shower before work, and look in the bathroom mirror. My hair is a matted mess as usual. I am normally not trying to impress anyone at work, but just in case Isabel shows up again, I better start trying a little harder to look presentable. I spot a couple new gray hairs and frown. My beard is getting long and a little out of hand. I am too skinny, and look sort of ridiculous with all of this hair set on such a thin frame.

I don't think I have trimmed my beard for about two months. A little kid at work last week yelled to his mom, "Look mommy, a ... hi ..., a hip ... ."

His mom asked what he wanted to say and he whispered to her, "I can't say it, it's a bad word." She leaned in as if to say it is OK, and the kid whispered in her ear, loud enough that I could still hear, "... A hipster." I glared at the kid, as a hipster would.

I guess I can't blame him. I examine the large black lines that form the sleeve tattoo that covers my entire left arm. In the center of my forearm, is a replica of the compass I gave my parents, a reminder, or a punishment I guess.

I brush the hair from my forehead. I normally keep it short around my ears and part it on the left side, sort of like Gramps does, now that I think of it. I have had the same hairstyle, apart from the beard, since I was a boy. I even still have the same cowlick on the top back part of my head, which always forces hair straight up in the air, as it does today.

I am cheap by necessity. Too cheap to get haircuts every

month, that is for sure. I only spend money on three things: good food, which most definitely includes good coffee; travel, when I can; and location, which explains why I live downtown in an overpriced apartment.

I love this city, although it is changing. People are moving to Denver in droves. When I ride my bike home from work, I always notice the license plates on the cars. Out of state plates seem to outnumber Colorado plates now. Just today, I spotted license plates from Florida, California, Texas, Georgia, Kansas, Wyoming, Washington, and Oregon.

People say traffic in the city is getting worse every day, but I wouldn't know. I do know how hard it is to find a lonely stretch of river to fish now, void of people, or how getting up I-70 into the mountains is a lesson in patience on a Friday afternoon. I will admit I may have cursed the foreigners' license plates from time to time, while stuck in traffic coming back home from the mountains on a Sunday afternoon.

While watching the news with Gramps last year, we saw a politician talking about building a wall between the United States and Mexico. Gramps turned to me and joked, "We should build a wall around Colorado, to keep everyone out." That wasn't the first time I had heard that joke. I reminded Gramps that technically, I wasn't born in Colorado either.

Because there is no wall yet, my rent will be increasing next month by almost $300 per month and I will likely have to move. I love this dump and, oddly, I don't want to move away from Gary downstairs. I don't have cable or even the internet. I don't own a car or pay for a parking spot. I also don't have a girlfriend, so I suppose being a loser saves me money. Any extra money I have goes to Gramps.

He thinks his water and electric bills are paid for by the "Senior Initiative of Colorado," an organization I invented out of thin air when I realized Gramps had less money than I do. Without me, he might end up like Gary.

A shower is too much work so I simply splash my face with some water and change out of my work clothes into sweatpants and a plain navy blue t-shirt. I am anxious to get started.

The book lying on the table in the living room could be the answer to my romantic drought. I hope it contains something, anything, that will help me find Isabel. I pick up the book and examine its cover, testing its weight like a rookie detective who has no idea what he is doing. It is thick, 448 pages, and heavy.

On the title page she has doodled a giant flower around the word *Andalusia*. I flip to a foldout map in the back of the book to see where exactly Andalusia is. Interesting. In the south of Spain. She has circled several cities on the map and drawn lines from Madrid to each of them. She labeled each line with a time. *2 horas. 4 horas. 6 horas.* Some of the lines even have prices sketched beside them. Maybe they are bus ticket prices or flights, I guess.

In the quick reference guide on the back of the front cover she has circled *Exchange Rates* and *Conversions*. The cities highlighted on the colored map of Andalusia include Córdoba, Sevilla, Ronda, Granada, Baeza, and Cádiz. I notice a coffee drip stain in the upper right corner of the map. This is my kind of girl.

My phone rings and I glance at the caller ID, though I don't need to. There are only two possibilities: work or Gramps. No one else ever calls me. The screen reads *Gramps* so I pick up.

"Hey, Gramps."

"Hi, Tiger," he says. "How was work?"

"Brilliant. What's up?"

"When are you coming fishing again?" he asks. "Next week right?"

Gramps is a constant joker. He once convinced me that Santa skipped our house because I liked salad. "Yep. Santa hates salad. Therefore, Santa hates you. You are out of luck," he told me with a perfect poker face. I believed him, too. He didn't cave until Mom let him have it.

"Very funny, Gramps," I say. "What are you up to today?"

He doesn't reply or laugh. There is only silence for a few seconds. I can almost hear him thinking. He coughs a few times into the phone.

"Gramps? You OK?" I ask.

"Are you coming fishing or not?" he asks, more firmly this time. He sounds annoyed.

"I was just up there last weekend. You almost got us killed. You mooned Jim. He shot at us. Don't you remember? I can't get away for another month or so, but it will be too cold by then. The river will probably be frozen over," I reply. Again, there is silence. I look at the screen to make sure I am still connected.

Finally, he replies, "Right. Last weekend. Well never mind. Have a good day, Tiger. Love you."

"Love you, too, Gramps. Are you OK?" I ask.

"I'm fine. Talk to you later," he says and hangs up the phone.

That was odd. I wonder what kind of joke Gramps is planning for me but I am also a little worried about him. He has seemed a bit "off" recently and overly forgetful. Gramps always jokes about dementia but lately those lighthearted comments are starting to scare me.

I stare back at the book, which seems to be watching me from the table. I almost don't want to open it again for fear of disappointment and a dead end. Sometimes hope seems like a better option than reality. First, I must drink coffee and have a snack.

My cupboard is full of different varieties of coffee, and I choose a strong dark roast from Cuba packed tightly in a bright yellow bag. I empty the old grounds from the filter holder of my espresso maker, grind the Cuban coffee beans, and pack the fresh grounds into the machine. I add water, flip it on, and watch the dark aromatic drops of dark coffee land in the small white espresso mug below.

The contents of the seasoned white fridge that came with this apartment always brighten my mood. Anything but a bachelor's fridge, it's filled with all kinds of culinary delights, like fresh veggies from the farmer's market around the corner, two kinds of eggs, quail and chicken, some prosciutto, three kinds of mustard, two strips of pepper bacon, some beets I pickled yesterday, and dough. As I grab the dough, I freeze with relief and disbelief.

Behind the dough, in the fridge, I spot my parents' compass. I must have placed it there absentmindedly and forgotten about it. I have been looking for that damn thing for weeks now, filled with anxiety, and all the while it was sitting in the fridge. Why did I put it there of all places?

A few tears trickle down my cheeks, but they don't surprise me as they used to. Crying, I have learned, can sneak up on you. I shake my head, wipe my eyes, and place the compass on the coffee table next to the guidebook, before getting to work in the kitchen.

I made the dough specifically for a French favorite of mine *pain au chocolat*. Mom's recipe. I find some dark chocolate in the cupboard and get to work, slowly rolling out the dough into thin layers and folding in bits of the dark chocolate. The pastries take shape as I roll them into recognizable treats. I pop them into the oven and leave them to bake for a few minutes.

The coffee is ready, and I take a sip, closing my eyes as I enjoy the bitter, almost smoky flavor. I grab a dark brown leather-bound notebook from the counter and scribble some notes about this coffee, how I made it, the date and my opinion.

9/21 — Cuban Dark Roast - Bitter. Strong. Smokey. Hint of roasted almond. Rating — 4/5. Possible feature.

I plan to use these notes someday to help me decide on the types of coffee to serve in my shop. It is my book of dreams.

I peek at the *pain au chocolat* in the oven, which are golden brown. There are bits of chocolate oozing out from both ends. I grab two and take them back to the table with my coffee.

I take a large bite as buttery flakes of the pastry and chocolate drip onto the cover of the book.

"Shit," I say and wipe it off with my sleeve. At the same time, I moan with delight. These gems taste like I plucked them from a shop in Paris.

I grab the book and open it again to the first page. I scanned the book earlier but clearly I have only scratched the surface. The book looks well used, and notes fill the margins of page after page. In these pages I hope to find some clues that will lead me to her. Maybe a phone number or an e-mail address of a friend or family member. Maybe her full name so as Gramps suggested, I can use "the Google" to find her.

Let the search of a madman begin.

CHAPTER FIVE

Every month I get a text from my Uncle Charlie that says the same thing: *I have a real job for you if you are ready.* I can count on the text almost like clockwork, but it still manages to piss me off with equal intensity every time. I never reply. I expect him to send another text soon.

Uncle Charlie, my mom's brother, means well, I know, but he is a smothering person whom I couldn't have less in common with. I know I should be grateful for his interest in my well-being, but I wish he would leave me alone. He has made it his mission to make sure I don't turn out like my mother. I think it must be his penance in life, his feeling sorry for me, the orphan of his sister, a sister I doubt he got along with even before I was born.

After Mom died, he sort of took it upon himself to make sure I was taken care of financially. Gramps certainly couldn't afford to pay for my college education, but Uncle Charlie could. He pushed me to go to college, even though I had no idea what I wanted to study, and generously offered to pay for it all.

I went to Western State University, in Gunnison, and majored in biology because that is what my great grandfather taught there. I didn't know what else to do. I quickly learned biology wasn't for me, so I dropped out my sophomore year. This led to a huge fight with Uncle Charlie when the truth came out. I told him that I wanted to travel for a while, like my parents had, to find myself, to find my path. Uncle Charlie said this was exactly what got them killed. He refused to let me live a "hippie dippy" lifestyle and die in the woods like some sort of directionless, homeless gypsy.

He couldn't understand why I had dropped out. He couldn't wrap his head around the lifestyle of a seeker. I wanted space to find answers before wasting Uncle Charlie's money on an education I wasn't sure I even wanted.

This all led to a family meeting at the cabin, where Uncle Charlie drilled me with questions. He paced back and forth in front of the fire while Gramps and I sat in the armchairs and listened. Gramps fidgeted with his fingernails, and I stared into the fire, letting the words pass through me. I heard the lecture but to me it had no meaning.

How are you going to get a job? Do you want to flip burgers or scrape by like your grandfather does? Do you want to do manual labor the rest of your life like all those damn Mexicans? You have to have a plan in life. What is your plan? Why in the hell do you think your answers are in some other foreign country? Why not change your major?

Uncle Charlie is a businessman. I don't think I have ever seen him in anything but a gray suit and a perfect black tie. His blond hair is always slicked back, and he has a large belly, a red face, and a veiny nose from too much whisky.

He is a wealthy man and lives in Texas on a giant ranch full of horses, cattle, and oil wells that provide him a hefty sum every month. I sometimes wonder how he and my mom were related. He has two kids, my cousins, whom I have never met, and a wife who looks like a Barbie doll.

If Uncle Charlie had his way I would take "safe" vacations like he does, sailing around the Caribbean on a giant cruise ship surrounded by sunburned tourists, overeating cheap food, and not risking a thing like death in the big bad woods.

We didn't speak for about a year after our family meeting at the cabin. He didn't convince me to change my major or go back to school. I drove around the country for a few months in my parents' old Volkswagen van before deciding to head to South America, where it was cheap and where adventure called. Not even Gramps was thrilled about this idea, but I went anyway.

There I fell in love with coffee. I volunteered on a plantation in Colombia in exchange for room and board, and spent four blissful months learning everything there is to know about Arabica beans and getting to know myself.

I learned how to plant, grow, cultivate, harvest, roast, and enjoy coffee. At that plantation, they practiced a traditional and natural way of processing coffee that is not very popular nowadays, but produces my favorite kind of brew.

I spent hours sweating in the hot humid landscape with the local workers, selectively picking the dried fruits from the trees. Handpicking only the best cherries is the slow way to go, and thus more expensive, but allows for a higher quality and more delicious final product.

I picked up a little Spanish during my time in Colombia, but not much. The local guys liked to teach me dirty words and laugh at my horrible pronunciation. I preferred to work hard in silence and spend long afternoons watching the sunset, sipping fresh coffee, and listening to the birds and howler monkeys scream from deep in the jungle. I was far away from home, which was exactly what I needed. It felt right to be there, lonely, but right.

When I finally returned to the United States, I was broke. Uncle Charlie got me a job working at an oil company in Denver. He was practically giddy when he flew to Denver to introduce me to his colleagues and saw me in a suit for the first time. He put his arm around my shoulder and said, "This is your path, Atlas, I promise you, this is where you are supposed to be." He guaranteed that I would thank him someday, and if I followed his lead, I would end up just fine.

I reluctantly settled into my new gray cube and collected large paychecks each month. I felt my soul slowly die. I would spend hours staring at my desk, doodling plans for the coffee shop that I would open someday.

I spent my work hours listening to Tanya, a bubbly brunette in her early 20s who sat in the cube next to mine. She would go on and on about her boyfriend, funny cat videos she watched all day, and I listened to her eat chips for hours. In the six months I worked there, she never asked me a single question. I would just listen to her talk at me, nodding every now and again, pretending to laugh when it was appropriate. Some days, I imagined her head exploding or that big dumb mouth of hers choking on salsa.

I hated it there. I hated everything about it. I hated my dusty black computer screen and the generic blue desktop company logo, which we were not allowed to change. I hated my boss, who would always greet me when I was a few minutes late in the morning by glancing at his gold watch.

We would have long meetings where we would stare at pointless graphs, and I would fidget in my monkey suit, uncomfortable as hell. I would have evaluations with my boss where he would explain that he didn't like my lack of enthusiasm. He wanted me to show more passion at work. It wasn't enough for me to just do my job. He wanted me to be more like Tanya. He wanted me to stay late sometimes, and show some ambition. He said I was an important part of the company, and if I put my mind to it, maybe in five years, I could become a manager.

Gramps encouraged me to quit. My happiness was all he wanted. He was a poor furniture maker though, and I liked the money I was earning.

I used that money to buy a top-of-the-line espresso machine and leather-bound notebooks, where I could keep detailed notes about the coffees I would feature someday in my coffee shop.

When I complained to Uncle Charlie that I didn't like the job, that I didn't feel it was right for me, he brushed it off and told me that "everyone has to work. Life can't be all rainbows and butterflies, you know. That is why they call it work." I told him about my dream of opening a coffee shop, and he told me to finish my degree, save up, and buy a franchise someday.

Gramps had raised me, and I valued his advice as he became my father figure. I would spend most weekends fishing with him near the cabin, and he would always tell me the same thing: "If this was your true path and purpose, you wouldn't feel so miserable. Success is not the size of your paycheck, it's about your happiness day to day."

As a furniture craftsman, he had managed to make ends meet for years and found enough happiness in it. Besides, 401(k)s are just an invention for money-hungry stock brokers and financial advisors to take your dough. At least that is what Gramps says. He keeps bags of cash buried all around the cabin, a "smart man's retirement plan."

After one fishing trip in particular, I overheard Gramps arguing with Uncle Charlie on the phone.

"Don't you think he should be happy?" Gramps had asked. "That boy has dealt with enough pain for a lifetime and, Goddammit, I am going to make sure he doesn't suffer anymore hardships."

I froze on the stairs of the cabin, afraid to move. Gramps hung up on Uncle Charlie and Grammy tried to calm him down.

"He has to be allowed to live, you can't shield him from everything," she said.

"I know, but I haven't seen that joy, that innocence in him, since they died," he said. "That boy is lost, and it's killing me. He is my responsibility and if he can't find his way, it's my fault."

I fought tears back then, but I couldn't help it. I cried silently on the stairs. Both Uncle Charlie and Gramps wanted me to be happy and had taken it upon themselves to make it so. The only problem was that they both had different ideas of what it meant to be content, and I had to figure out what happiness was for myself.

A year passed and the oil company gave me a one-year anniversary card to commemorate my year of hard work. I stared at that card, depressed, sitting in my gray cube. Tanya looked at the card, ate a chip, and proceeded to tell me about her weekend. I felt like an actor in my own life. What was I doing here? An entire year, wasted. For what?

In that moment, I saw the depth of time that had passed, and it terrified me. I quit before the future could gobble me up.

Gramps couldn't have been more supportive. I still remember what he said to me.

"It's just a job, Tiger. Don't do what society tells you to do. Do what you feel is right in your soul. The money will come," he had said.

Upon the news of my resignation from my oil job, Uncle Charlie made another surprise visit to the cabin where I was spending the weekend fishing with Gramps to celebrate the death of the monkey suit. When he got there, World War III exploded in the living room.

"You are both losers. I just don't understand how you two can be satisfied with so little," Uncle Charlie said. "I mean, look at your old truck out there. It's as good as dead. The roof needs repairs, and you can barely afford gas. And Atlas, you have to borrow cars from your friends. I mean, really?"

"I make what little I have work for me. Money isn't everything," Gramps said.

"That's great on a bumper sticker, but money *is* everything. Without it you can't do anything. Since you lazy bums don't want to work, I am pretty sure you will both be homeless soon. Then what? Then you are going to call me asking for help. Let me tell you I just *love* giving money to people who aren't willing to work for themselves."

"Gramps owns this cabin, you moron," I said. "We won't be

homeless."

"You have him defending your lifestyle now? You are encouraging irresponsibility, you know. His dad would never have approved. You are a poor substitute for a father," Uncle Charlie said.

"And how often do you see your own kids, Charlie? Once or twice a week? Or are you making that money on business trips all the time? You are so busy earning money that you don't have time to spend with the people you love," Gramps said.

"Stop talking, old man," Uncle Charlie whispered.

"You think talking on the phone with your kids is good enough? It's sad really. Your values are all out of whack. How can you fault Atlas for wanting a job he enjoys? He wants to open a coffee shop of his own. That is his dream. Is that so bad?"

"Do you think I *enjoy* traveling for work all the time? No! But I do it because I am a man, and I provide for my family!" Heavy breathing filled the room. Both their faces were red, frothing at the mouths like wolves fighting to the death in the wild.

"Well your kids don't care if you are a man. They care if you are present. They won't remember how many toys you gave them or how big the house was that you lived in. They will remember if you were there. If you showed up. If you think I'm a poor substitute for a father then I really think you should look in the mirror," Gramps said.

Uncle Charlie's final words to the both of us were, "You are not my problem now. Don't call me ever again."

To which Gramps replied, "You are a true Texan now, you entitled little shit!"

I started working at Speedy Coffee after that. Despite the fact that we don't get along, the truth is that Uncle Charlie is always in the back of my head informing my decisions. I can't help but think he may be right. Maybe that is why I feel so foolish for chasing stupid dreams.

I hear him in the back of my head now as I dream of finding Isabel. *Is this a foolish quest? Is this a waste of time?* I know he would say yes and tell me to go on some real dates like a real man. He would tell me I have my head in the clouds again. He would tell me that the only reason I want to find her is because she is just out of reach. He would ask me how dreaming has worked out for me thus far. The answer would be not well.

Unfortunately the cynical voices in life tend to drown out that inner whisper of truth.

My phone buzzes.

I have a real job for you if you are ready.

CHAPTER SIX

I scan each page of the guidebook like I'm Sherlock Holmes. I am looking for anything at all that might indicate a way for me to find Isabel. I take a sip of my espresso, which has gone cold.

The first page of the guidebook is an introduction to Spain. I pull out a small piece of paper wedged between pages three and four: a receipt, which is acting as a bookmark. The receipt indicates that she purchased the book over a month ago at the Tattered Cover Bookstore in Denver. Whatever she is planning or decision she has made must have been a recent one. I now have the last four digits of her credit card number, but I doubt that will help me find her. I would be able to match the number to our records at Speedy Coffee, but I was flirting and gave her the coffee for free.

The pages of the introduction to Spain are crisp as it appears she has skipped this part. I don't blame her. A Spanish girl hardly needs an introduction to Spain.

She has dog-eared several pages in the Sevilla section and the Granada section. In the margins, I find stars and circles. On a page called *48 Hours in Granada*, she has written *wifi-CooC4321*, no doubt a password for internet at some coffee shop likely somewhere else in Denver.

She has also starred the word *Ronda* and underlined the description: *Perched on an inland plateau river by the 100m fissure of El Tajo Gorge, Ronda is Málaga province's most spectacular town.*

In the Sevilla section, she has circled several restaurants, *Los Coloniales, Uinería San Telmo,* and *Las Navezuelas.* She has written seven exclamation points around *Las Navezuelas.* The description *Homegrown produce rules the roost of this wonderful* finca *(farm) restaurant* is circled and she has written *que significa 'rules the roost'* above it, clearly unfamiliar with English slang.

It looks like my kind of place. "Maybe I will get to try it with her someday," I mumble. I flip to another page. "Sure you will, you idiot."

A few hours pass as I continue to investigate the book. I am so engrossed in my activity that I fail to notice the time until I see it has gotten dark outside.

I turn my attention again to the maps in the book. Isabel has dog-eared several neighborhoods in Sevilla and Granada. I study a map that looks like she used over and over again, the corners of the pages worn slightly more than the rest of the book.

The maps of El Arenal and Triana in Sevilla are particularly worn. She has circled *Plaza Nueva* and written *expensive* next to this area. She has circled *Plaza de Toros de la Real* and drawn a sad face next to the words. She has also circled an area from the *Rio Guadalquivir* down *Avenida la Republica Argentina* to *Calle San Jacinto.* She has circled the word *Triana* and doodled a star and a smiley face next to this neighborhood. Her black question mark looms large in the center of the page like an omen.

I flip to the Granada map for comparison. She has highlighted sections of this city map. I see an *X* with *el mercado* written next to it. She has circled the street *Acera del Darro* from the *Puerta Real* and several city blocks in this area. I freeze.

A phone number. At least I think it is a phone number. My eyes examine the numerals, three of them inside parentheses and what appears to be a country code. *Should I call the number?* But as quickly as it came, my excitement drains from my body as a thought pops into my head. *Why would you write your own phone number in a guidebook?* The answer to that question is of course, you wouldn't.

She has also circled the Albayzin neighborhood and doodled hearts on the Alhambra. I turn the page and find more phone numbers written in the margins.

Why would I write phone numbers in a guidebook? They are not for restaurants or hotels because those numbers are already listed.

I try to recall more information from our brief conversation. The 30-minutes that have turned me into a crazy person. I go through my mental checklist for clues, playing back that night like a broken VHS tape full of dark gaps and static.

She is from Spain. She plays the guitar and loves coffee. She was on vacation when I met her, and it was her first time in the U.S. "Isabel. Pleasure to meet you, Atlas Green," she had said, and she actually seemed pleased to meet me. I remember her eyes, or rather the person, the soul behind those eyes, made my entire body fill with warmth.

She had brown, straight shoulder-length hair. She had dark brown eyes and wore no makeup, or at least no makeup that I could detect. She was confident, but in a modest way. She laughed when I made jokes about espresso, and she was wearing a fluffy, colorful scarf.

She gave me her number and said, "It should be good for a little while longer. Text, don't call." She kept fidgeting with her coffee cup when I gave it to her and looking down at her hands. I remember her hands because each of her fingernails were painted different colors, like a pack of Skittles and she was wearing a virtual rainbow of bracelets around both of her wrists.

I also remember annoying myself. I couldn't stop saying, "For sure, yeah for sure, for sure," over and over again, like some kind of simpleton.

Maybe the number she gave me was temporary or something, since she was traveling. I decide I need a second opinion and call Gramps.

"Hello, Tiger," he answers after the first ring.

"How did you know it was me?" I ask.

"Unless your grandmother is calling me from the grave, it'd be you," he replies.

"Hey, do you remember that girl I told you about?" I ask, hoping he isn't keeping up the joke from our last conversation.

"Yeah. You forgot or lost her phone number, right? And now you are stalking her," he says with a laugh.

"Yeah, that's the one. I found some phone numbers written next to maps in a guidebook she left at the coffee shop. Why would a person write phone numbers in a guidebook and circle neighborhoods?" I ask.

"Because she is clearly a hooker, a fine dish. Client numbers of course." He chuckles. "Maybe you should have given her *your* number. You would be having a grand old time right now."

"Are you finished?"

"It's no mystery, Charlie," Gramps says.

"Charlie? This is Atlas," I correct him.

"Did I say Charlie?" he continues. "Tiger. I used to do the same with newspapers and a map. That is what people used to do before your internet came along. She is apartment hunting. She is looking for a place to live. It's as simple as that."

I sigh. I am a little embarrassed at the obviousness of the answer.

"Thanks, Gramps," I say.

"And I'm sure she is an angel," he says. "The opposite of a hooker. Love you, Tiger."

"Did you eat?" I ask before he can hang up.

"Not the gourmet stuff you probably did, but yeah, I ate," he says. "It's pork and beans night here at the castle."

We say our goodbyes and hang up. I spend the next few hours examining every inch of the guidebook. I want to make sure I don't miss a thing. When I have finished, and turned the last page, the only thing I know is that she is apartment hunting in Sevilla and Granada. I have no idea which city she has chosen or even when she is planning this move. I don't even know for sure if she is moving. I toss the book on my ugly, tattered, orange thrift store couch in frustration and glance at the clock, which reads 11:00 p.m.

I have no idea what my next move should be. I only know I feel restless. I can feel a change coming and I can't shake it.

CHAPTER SEVEN

"It's for you," Amanda says, handing me the phone. She goes back to pouring caramel into a cup.

I give her a confused look. No one has ever called me on the work phone.

"This is Atlas," I say while plugging my opposite ear to block out the noise of the busy coffee shop.

"Yes. Hello, Atlas," an official sounding female voice cuts through the line. "I'm afraid I have some bad news."

"What is it?" I ask.

"My name is Officer Sarah Piedmont, and it's about your grandfather," the woman says.

"What happened?" The blood drains from my body. I feel light-headed. Amanda sees the expression on my face and puts her hand on my shoulder.

"I'm afraid he has been arrested," Officer Piedmont explains in a robotic voice. "He was at the grocery store in Gunnison and caused quite a scene. He was not cooperating so we had to bring him down to the station. He wanted us to call his wife, but our records indicate she is deceased. He finally gave us your number."

"OK. What can *I* do?" The volume of my voice raises slightly, betraying my attempt to remain calm.

Her voice softens a little, and she replies, "Well, he is really angry, but if you ask me, he is just confused. It happens sometimes at this age. I offered to take him home but he can't seem to remember his address."

I freeze for what must have been an awkward amount of time. I don't know what to do or say. My mouth is dry, like I have a mouthful of coffee grounds.

"Hello? Atlas, are you there?" Officer Piedmont asks.

"Can I give you the address, and you can take him home?" I reply.

"Of course, but is there anyone at home to help him?" she asks.

"No. He lives alone but I guess, well, I live in Denver, so it will take me four or five hours to get there. I will take off work and drive over. Do you think he is OK to be alone for a while?" I ask.

"He should be fine," she says.

"OK. Thanks. Is that all?"

"Well no. There is a small fine from the arrest," she says flatly. "It's two hundred dollars. How will that be paid?"

"Two *hundred* dollars! Why don't you spend your time arresting *real* criminals!" I yell before thinking. Amanda is biting her nails and staring at me. She loves gossip and is practically chomping at the bit for me to get off the phone and tell her what is going on.

"Yes. Two hundred dollars," the officer says again. "Payment is due by the first of the month. I will leave the citation with your grandfather."

I hang up on her without responding. I can't afford this. Neither can Gramps. I feel panic, anger, sadness, and confusion pulse through me all at the same time.

"Are you OK?" Amanda asks, placing her hand on my shoulder again. She bites her lower lip and her eyes ask for an explanation.

"I have to leave. Gramps has been arrested. I have to go. Can you cover for me?" I ask.

"Of course, Atlas. It's no problem," she says. "Can I help? What can I do?"

"No. I just. I have to go," I say. I take off my green apron and stuff it into my bag. "Actually, yes. Can I borrow your car? I'm really sorry. I just, I can't afford to rent one right now. I will fill the tank when I get back."

Amanda pauses before she concedes. "I guess. Sure," she says and hands me the keys.

I hate being in debt to people, and borrowing a car is one of those things that makes me feel poor. I locate Amanda's car, a blue 1980-something Honda Civic, and hop in. Pink fuzzy dice hang from the rear-view mirror and the car smells like fruity perfume and hairspray.

I try to take a deep breath as I argue with myself. *Why can't someone else deal with Gramps? This isn't fair. My parents should be around for this. Uncle Charlie should be around for this.* My anger only starts to ease up when worry pushes it aside. One thought repeats itself over and over again in my head: *What is wrong with Gramps?*

I stop by my apartment and illegally double park outside. Gary is there, as usual, sitting on a cardboard box. He is drinking cheap whisky and slurs his words when he sees me. "Hey, whadleyoursay, Atlas. Did your brang meey coffee?"

"Gary. Make sure no one tows the car, OK?" I say as I rush past him.

"Your gotter," he replies, accepting his mission.

I run up the stairs to grab some clothes, my phone charger, and my toothbrush. I spot the guidebook and compass on the table and decide to bring them along. I check the stove and everything in the apartment to make sure switches are turned off and quickly head back out the door.

"Heeey the mannnn looks mad," Gary slurs to me.

The person whom I have double parked next to and boxed in is glaring at me.

"C'mon, man. Hurry up!" He holds his hand down on the horn and doesn't let up.

"Take it easy," I reply. "Give me a second."

Gary is screaming at the man and giving him the finger. I can't help but grin as I jump in the car and speed away.

In a daze I dart through downtown traffic and onto Highway 285, which slowly takes me west into the mountains. I struggle to settle in for the long drive to Gunnison.

What is wrong with Gramps? What is wrong with Gramps? The thought is a persistent one and so strong it is almost tangible. The *what ifs* and the worry drive me half mad.

What if he has lost his mind? What if he needs to move? What if he can't live alone anymore? What if he has more police incidents? What if he has medical bills? What if he dies? And the worst *what if* of them all: *What if he has dementia, or even worse, Alzheimer's? What then?*

It is the first time I have thought of Gramps as anything but my grandfather. He has always been someone who will forever be there. He is my best friend and someone I talk to all the time. He has never really had any health problems, at least nothing he has told me about. He is my protector, my safety net, my person. Now it seems *I* might be charged with caring for *him*.

I pass through Johnson Village and admire the giant fourteener Mount Sneffels to my right. The sun is beginning to set, and huge puffs of clouds light up into a million hues of orange and pink above the snowcapped mountain peaks. In this area the blue spruce have given way to juniper trees and red dirt, which seem to mirror the colors in the air. The moon has appeared in the twilight, and as I drive, the colors slowly fade to navy blue, then to dark purple, the sky the color of juniper berries. It is impossible to pass these mountains without thinking of my parents, who disappeared somewhere, up there, in those woods.

Amanda's car struggles up Monarch Pass. The headlights capture the pavement which slowly cuts through a dense pine forest. I am mindful of deer as I have hit a few in the past while driving through these mountains. I roll down the window; the handle creaks and protests as the cold fall air tumbles inside, blowing the fuzzy pink dice around in circles.

It is an odd thing to sense this monumental role reversal, as I begin to think more and more of myself taking care of Gramps. Sure, I have paid some of his bills for a while, but he has always been my rock. Sometimes it seems he is the only thing in my life that I can count on.

I shake my hands in the car, trying to get rid of the feeling. Gramps is too young for this. This is only supposed to happen to other people who don't take care of themselves.

Why me? It seems unfair. I am not rich. I am a loser by many accounts, and I don't have anyone to help me. I don't have siblings to call. Uncle Charlie will probably send a check, but he never shows up when it gets tough. The barrage of self-pity makes me feel guilty. Gramps is the one that this situation will really hurt. I need to stop being so selfish.

After a few more hours, I finally spot the bright lights of the McDonald's sign up ahead to my right, and eventually the giant white *W* made out of rock to my left, which takes up most of the small hillside upon entering town. The *W* is illuminated by moonlight. I am thankful and at the same time anxious that I have finally arrived.

The gas needle is approaching empty, so I pull into the gas station on the outskirts of town. The dash clock in the car reads 8:45 p.m. I blow air into my hands as I fill up the car. Gunnison is always the coldest place in Colorado, and it always shocks your system when you arrive. I spot a sign advertising gas station coffee and shake my head. I'm in a terrible mood, and I managed to forget to eat today.

I grab a bag of almonds inside the florescent-lit gas station. A large woman behind the counter recites a sales pitch I am sure her boss requires. Her lack of enthusiasm is obvious. I recognize it all too well.

"Can I interest you in a decaf pumpkin spiced latte?" she robotically says as she rings up my almonds. She sounds like me, pushing green tea lattes on people, secretly hoping they don't order that funk.

"No, thank you. You couldn't pay me to drink that," I mutter under my breath.

She stares at me without losing eye contact and flashes a perfectly robotic smile. She hands me my change. Her nametag says Martha.

"Have a nice day," she says, waving like a beauty pageant winner from hell as I head out the door.

I hop back in the car and make my way through the center of town. Gunnison is a small town, and I feel like I know most of the families that live here. I slowly crawl past the park next to Western State University, where my great grandfather taught Biology and I spent two years of my life. I turn right on Main Street past the family-owned Sweet Pea Ice Cream. It is closed at this hour, but the neon sign is still turned on in the window.

My grandparents used to take me to Sweet Pea for ice cream all the time when I was a kid to get huge Palisade Peach ice cream cones and to shoot the breeze with the owners. Every time I see them now they always look astonished and tell me that they remember when I was still "pissin' in my pants."

I drive past the general store, where Gramps always buys his lawnmower parts, bolts, and other miscellaneous items he needs to assemble the furniture he makes. The store stocks everything you need for an old cabin: mousetraps, varnish, chicken wire, WD-40, mothballs, fishing line, fishing hooks, worms, camping chairs, coolers, pancake mix, paint, matches, and even pickles.

The store has survived despite a large Walmart that opened

right across the street. Gramps refuses to shop in the shiny new Walmart, and he promises Mr. Craner, who has owned the general store since the flood, that he will never defect. I associate the store with impatience, as every time we visit for a nail or some other odd thing, it takes an hour to get out of there. Gramps and Mr. Craner gossip together like two teenagers.

I head out of town and turn on the road towards Baldwin, where Gramps waits. The road is paved for a while, and then turns to dirt where the farmland gives way to national forest. The car vibrates as I drive over bumpy roads, and I slow the car to a stop when two shiny eyes appear in the darkness, reflecting my headlights. A large deer steps out onto the road in front of me. Enormous antlers protrude from his head, regal and strong. He stares at me for a while, in a trance, and I turn off my headlights and the car, to let him pass.

When my eyes adjust to the darkness, I spot five female deer emerging from the woods and walk onto the road. Their breath is visible in the cold moonlit air, and they take their time crossing. I roll my window down slowly to watch them walk into a large meadow on the opposite side of the road before turning the car back on and facing the inevitable.

When I finally pull onto the dirt road leading up to the cabin, instead of the comfort at the site of Joe Peanut's grave welcoming me to my favorite place in the world, I am filled with anxiety and sadness.

A soft glow from the lights inside of the cabin trickles out into the darkness, and I catch a glimpse of Gramps through the front window. He isn't reading or watching TV. He is simply staring at a spot on the floor in front of him, lost in a forest of thoughts. For the briefest of moments I don't recognize him and quickly realize it is because Gramps is always smiling around me. Worry is worn like a mask on his face.

I knock once and open the door, which isn't locked. "Gramps, I'm here. Why don't you lock the door?" I ask, hoping the

Gramps I have always known will greet me.

"Hey ,Tiger. The cop said you would be here," he grumbles.

I can see him struggling to smile, fighting his own unease, trying to put his face of strength on for me. The lines in his skin look extra dark and gray tonight.

"What happened?" I ask, grabbing a seat next to him on my leather armchair in front of the fireplace. The living room is cold and unusually messy. Packaging from TV dinners are strewn about the room and a half-eaten apple, brown, and rotting rests on the floor. Suddenly Gramps slams his fist on the arm of his chair, causing some dirty dishes on the side table to rattle.

"I was minding my own business when that damn cop got me all riled up!" he complains.

"What happened before that?" I ask, my voice soft enough to calm him.

"I was grocery shopping and must have forgotten my wallet in the trunk. I told the cashier I would be right back and then ... and then I forgot where I parked," he replies. I can't stop looking around the room while he talks.

It is so depressing, thinking about Gramps living here all alone, no one around for miles, eating frozen dinners and watching TV. I need to do something, so I make a fire, as if that will dispel the loneliness in the room and the guilt engulfing me. Gramps continues his version of the day's events as I carefully stack small sticks and bits of kindling in a teepee shape over balled up newspapers.

"The next thing I know, there is a cop telling me I need to go pay for my groceries. So I tell her to piss off. To mind her own business, and all of a sudden I'm in the can. Can you believe it? They arrested a harmless old man." Gramps clenches his teeth and balls up his fist as if ready for a fight.

I light the fire and watch the small green flames turn to blue and then orange as they lick their way up the paper and ignite the wood. Smoke curls its way up into the chimney.

"Did the cop leave a note or anything?" I ask. Gramps points to the coffee table. I grab the envelope from the table and read my name on the front. *Atlas Green.*

Inside the envelope I find the bill. It is for two hundred dollars as promised, for public disruption. The description of his offense is printed in a box at the bottom. This is the account from the officer's point of view:

I was called to the scene at approximately 11:01 a.m. An elderly individual was yelling at a grocery store manager. He was accusing the store manager of stealing his car. He shoved a grocery store clerk and I took appropriate action to place the individual in my squad car where he was then taken to the station. With the keys and car description from the individual, we were able to locate the car in question, which was still in the grocery store parking lot.

I spot a small handwritten note inside the envelope scribbled on the back of a blank yellow speeding ticket.

Atlas,
I am sorry about all of this. On a personal note, my grandfather has Alzheimer's disease so I know how difficult this can be. Let me know if I can help in any way.
Sincerely,
Officer Sarah Piedmont

I grab some large logs and place them carefully on the fire. Alzheimer's. Shit. Shit. Shit. I am struggling to catch my breath. Somehow seeing someone else describe Gramps in this way confirms my worst fears. Her words have made it seem real and plunge me into a reality I don't want to acknowledge. I squeeze and crumple the note and toss it into the fire, watching it slowly burn.

CHAPTER EIGHT

The smell of coffee wakes me. It fills the air like a rich perfume. I forget where I am for a moment and look around the room through half open eyes. There is frost on the inside of the old glass window next to my bed. My bare feet hit the cold wood floor and I take a deep breath. For a brief moment my worries have left me, cleansed from my mind by sleep.

I look outside the window of my room and take in a bright, sunshine-filled Colorado morning. Snow has fallen overnight on the mountain tops that surround the valley. The sea of emerald green sage bushes that fill Baldwin look vibrant and clean. A few woodchucks call out, their chirps echoing off the walls of the empty crumbling cabins that surround us.

I grab my green plastic compass, flip open the top, place it on my pillow and watch it slowly spin for a while as I lie on my side in the bed. When I first moved in with Grammy and Gramps, we spent the first few months trying to fix the compass. Gramps, of course, thought I just loved the thing. I have always been obsessed with the compass, but what Gramps doesn't know is that it's more a reminder of the guilt I feel about my parents' death than a treasured memento.

Together Gramps and I learned that Earth is a magnet itself.

It is a cosmic force that can interact with other magnets. It is this unseen energy, an unchanging guide for all things that causes, or is *supposed* to cause, a compass to point us in the right direction.

I have somehow always drawn comfort from this phenomenon. No matter where you stand on Earth—Australia, Fiji, Colombia, Spain or Colorado—your compass will point to the North Pole. If you are lost, you should always be able to find home.

When Grammy and Gramps drove me to the bus stop for my first day of school after my parents disappeared, they had gotten into an argument about where exactly the bus stop was. Gramps told her that he had iron boogers, which made her roll her blue eyes and smack him on the shoulder. I remember taking this very seriously and asking him what he meant.

He explained that men have iron boogers, which makes them better at directions, especially while driving. It's like having a compass in your nose. Grammy told me not to pay any attention to the old fool. They laughed a lot. I was glad they both had the magic, too.

I got beat up that day by a fat kid with freckles named Jonathan Hill. He was as dumb as a cow pie, but he had gone through puberty earlier than the rest of us and was practically a giant. His parents were dead too. He sat on me and gave me a bloody nose. I never understood what it was about me that made him so mad. He never gave me a second look when my parents were alive.

I swallowed a small magnet when I got home from school that day. I don't know why exactly. I just put it in my mouth and swallowed. I suppose I thought it would help guide me through this world somehow and help steer clear of Jonathan Hill. I told Gramps I now had an iron stomach, just like his iron boogers, which got Gramps in big trouble with Grammy, and earned me a trip to the hospital.

Gramps and I painstakingly took my plastic compass apart

again and again. The small magnetic needle is supposed to be well balanced on a frictionless pivot point in the middle. Our guess was that the compass could never find north, because there was something keeping it from spinning correctly, an unseen tilt of some kind. We thought maybe there was a speck of dust or a foreign object causing it to malfunction.

We used tweezers and a red Swiss Army knife, spending hours in front of the fireplace downstairs, trying to fix the compass. I would get so frustrated when, after taking it apart, spraying the balance point in the middle with oil and then reassembling it again, it would continue to spin, never landing on north. Gramps would piss and moan, too.

I could always tell when Gramps was really mad by the curse words he chose. When he was only sort of mad he would say "gosh darn't," or occasionally "shit," which always made me giggle. When he was really ticked off he would yell, "Judas Priest." I thought for the longest time that Judas was a planet in our solar system. I received harsh feedback from school for filling in the question, *What is the 9th planet in our solar system?* with *Judas*.

Grammy really let Gramps have it for that. She said, "You are a real stubborn son of a bitch sometimes, Charles Green." She never cursed, so I knew she was extra mad. The very last time we tried to fix the compass, Gramps yelled "Judas Priest," and chucked it across the room. To this day you can still make out the crack in the outer plastic shell from Gramps's tantrum.

I think he wanted more than anything for me to smile. I was sad, and understandably so, for many years after my parents vanished in the woods. Gramps tried everything to cheer me up.

We played the trumpet together, an interest of mine, and something Gramps was actually quite good at. He owned several beautiful silver Bach Stradivarius trumpets, and he would turn on the large old brown wooden radio in the cabin, which is about the size of a small refrigerator, sit downstairs next to the fire and listen to jazz on the AM dial.

He would listen to a few songs, just sitting there holding the trumpet and tapping his foot. He especially loved Miles Davis, Louis Armstrong, and Cootie Williams. Grammy would give me strawberry candies and tell me to go help him. I never knew what to do exactly, but I would sit next to him, sucking on my candies, and watch him lose himself in the music.

His eyes would remain closed, his bare foot tapping to the tune. If I tried to speak, he would just hold up a hand for silence. Around the third song, he would always raise the trumpet to his lips, blow spit out of the spit valve, and begin to play. His eyes would always remain shut, but he would play along with the radio, adding his tune.

One day I picked up one of his trumpets and tried to play along with him. An awful, goose-like noise came out the other end, but Gramps saw that it made me smile. That was all he needed.

"Morning, Tiger," Gramps says as I step down the creaky stairs into the kitchen.

"Gramps, your cheeks are red and my nose is running. It's freezing in here. You want me to make a fire?" I ask as I rub my hands together for warmth. Gramps is wearing white long johns and a blue wool winter hat that engulfs his head and covers his ears. He looks prepared for Antarctica.

"Knock yourself out. I'm making pancakes. You want some?" he asks.

"Sure," I say as I grab a steaming cup of coffee and start making a fire. Gramps hums jazz to himself as he cooks.

"I read your book," he says.

"What book?"

"The guidebook for Spain. The one from our lover girl."

I look over at the counter in the kitchen. He must have grabbed my things from the car this morning. The guidebook, which is now filled with little yellow Post-it notes, sits on top of an old coffee can. The notes stick out from all sides of the book, making it look like it has sprouted leaves.

"It looks like you made a few discoveries," I say as the fire catches and begins to blaze. I rub my hands together again and face both hands, palms down, towards the fire, which slowly begins to warm the room.

Gramps sets down a plate filled with piping hot pancakes on the table next to the kitchen. He grabs some syrup and sets it on the table along with a stick of butter.

I grab the syrup and can't help myself. "Gramps, this stuff is fake. You know that, right?"

"Yes, but it tastes like real syrup, and it only cost me two dollars," he says, laughing. "Eat it, you picky city boy."

We both sit down at the table. This is my second favorite spot in the cabin, runner-up to the fireplace. The large round wooden table, which Gramps built, sits in front of a giant window offering an amazing view of the ghost town of Baldwin and the valley below. The best part of the view are the snowcapped mountains towering all around us.

I take a bite of my chocolate chip and banana filled pancake. This is the signature dish of bachelor Gramps. The pancakes are hot and delicious, and they pair perfectly with the generic store brand coffee. I know this coffee is the cheap kind, filled with 15% un-roasted coffee beans, but it is still good. I smile at Gramps.

He smiles back, "Pretty good. I told you."

The tension from last night is gone. Gramps is avoiding the subject, and I appreciate the distraction.

"Hey, what do you think about going fishing? We should go catch us some dinner at dusk," Gramps says with his mouth full of pancake.

"Sure. As long as you don't reveal your butt again," I say. "I'm scarred for life, ya know."

Gramps bursts into wild laughter. I can't help but join in. The relief of a lighthearted morning washes over us and refreshes our spirits.

I pick up the guidebook. "So, you found my Spanish girl?"

Gramps smiles slyly. He seems to have answers.

"Your old grandad is not as dumb as he looks," he says. "You can thank me at your wedding. Give me that." I hand him the book. "Look here," he says flipping the pages of the book until he finds the note he is looking for. "I noticed a lot of doodles," he says.

"Doodles?" I mumble, my mouth full of pancake.

"Yes, doodles," he replies as a matter of fact.

"See? Look," he says, pointing to some scribbles that have formed a flower on one page, then a smiley face on the next. He flips to another to show me spirals that look like pasta in the margins of the book.

"Doodles," he explains. "Your grandmother and mother used to doodle on everything."

I always notice the pain in his face when my mom comes up in conversation. "Is doodling your big discovery?" I say, impatiently wanting him to get to the point.

"Doodling is a sign, a clue, about personality," he says. "Your mom used to doodle flowers, which means she was happy. Your grandmother used to draw hearts when she was yapping on the phone. When she was mad at me, she would draw angry-looking black circles."

I get up to place another log on the fire as Gramps continues. "My point is that this girl is happy. You don't want to go searching for some girl that doodles zombies or vampires or knives would you?" he asks.

"I guess not," I reply sitting back down at the table. Gramps takes a big sip of coffee before he continues.

"I have confirmed what I told you before, about her apartment hunting," he says. "She is either moving to Sevilla or Granada." Gramps smiles with satisfaction. "I also noticed this."

He holds up a piece of paper that has an internet password written on it. He looks pleased with himself and hands it to me. The paper is about half the size of a bookmark. I examine it and the password she has written on it. Her handwriting is neat and somehow friendly. I smell the paper, which smells a little bit like coffee and perfume. Or, at least I think so. The smell is so faint that it could also be my imagination.

"It smells good," I say.

"It's a good thing you are a barista," Gramps says. "Look." He points to the bottom of the paper. Printed in small letters is the name of a business.

Café Fútbol – Plaza de Mariana Pineda 6 – Granada

She has clearly torn this from a business notepad.

"So what?" I say returning the piece of paper to Gramps. "So she was at this café at some point in her life. Big deal."

"You have to go there, genius."

"That's crazy talk," I say.

"Did you see the best doodle of all?"

"I don't follow, Gramps. There are a lot of scribbles in the book."

He flips to a page near the back of the book and opens it wide before placing it in front of me and pointing to the scribble he is referring to. I feel joy jump out of nowhere and electrify me. I can't believe it. Gramps is grinning from ear to ear and pumping his bushy gray eyebrows up and down in his best lover-boy look. I don't know how I missed this before.

Isabel has sketched a small heart in blue ink. The heart is surrounded by question marks and, in the middle of the heart, she has written the letters *AG*.

"Atlas Green!" Gramps yells and slams his hand on the table, causing the pancakes and syrup bottles to jump in the air. "Your mom used to do that when she was in middle school. She picked some muscular young stud she liked and doodled hearts and initials till blisters stopped her."

Gramps clasps his hands together and pumps his eyebrows up and down again, trying his best Isabel impression, which sounds more like a southern girl who guzzled a gallon of varnish and washed it down with whisky. "I do declare, Atlas Green, also known as AG, will be my hot handsome stud of a husband someday. Yes, yes, I do declare."

"She is not from Alabama, Gramps. Good lord."

"You have to go. You have to, Atlas. Go find her in Spain," he says in his normal voice.

"I can't, Gramps. It's ... it's just not a good time," I awkwardly shift in my chair.

Gramps takes another long sip of his coffee. His hands cup the mug for warmth as he stares out the window without speaking. He waits a few minutes before saying anything.

"Your grandmother was the best thing that ever happened to me," he says. "I wonder what life would have been like without her. If I had married someone else. Or if I had never married anyone at all."

Grammy died in her sleep a few years ago. The doctors said it was "old age," which caused Gramps to punch a hole in the hospital wall. He said they were just being lazy and didn't want to find the real cause because we were poor.

I follow his eyes outside to watch a hummingbird whir up to the bright red feeder hanging from the windowsill above. The hummingbird darts and stops to take a drink of the sugar water in the feeder. His neck is ruby red and the side of his body shimmers green. He slowly guides his tiny needlelike beak into the center of a plastic yellow flower, withdrawing the liquid inside.

Hummingbirds were Grammy's favorite. There is still a poster hung on the wooden wall next to the window that labels all of the different types of hummingbirds in Colorado. Gramps may not remember to feed himself sometimes, but he always remembers to feed those birds.

"Love is an odd thing. People will tell you that relationships and marriages are hard. But it never was for me. I swear to you, it never was." Gramps turns his gaze back to me. His eyes are clear, brown, and focused.

"Your grandmother was like, well, being with her was like sitting in a boat and floating downstream. When you know you know. I didn't have a paddle, I didn't need one. It just worked. It was just natural. Your parents had the same thing. Lightning struck our family twice. Do you understand what I'm saying?" he asks.

"I do, but I don't know what that's like, Gramps," I reply. "I think you got lucky. The rest of us have to live in the real world, with real relationships."

Gramps shakes his head. Perhaps at my cynical view of love. "Tiger, what I'm saying is when you see the boat, you damn well better do everything in your power to get in it. You can't just be like most people who just watch the boat float away, pointing, without ever taking action. Then they spend their lives in a state of coulda, shoulda, woulda. You don't want to be like that."

I think about my past relationships. There was Rachel. We dated for four months until I couldn't take the smell of her perfume or annoying laugh anymore. My longest was Allison, which lasted six months. I was the dumped one in that relationship. I was probably too clingy, and she said I chewed too loudly. She also said being a barista is not a real profession. She wanted someone who could make "adult money."

The rest of my girlfriends, if you could call them that, lasted a few weeks at a time, always ending mutually. I am starting to seriously think something must be wrong with me. I now *expect* them all to fail, from the very beginning. My love life is a self-fulfilling prophecy.

"But, Gramps, I only met Isabel once. I don't know much about her at all and she lives in another country," I say.

"You know how I met your grandmother, right?" Gramps always beams with joy when he tells this story. I nod.

"I went to pick up her sister to take her out for a soda, and your grandmother answered the door instead. I just sat there all dumb like, with my jaw hanging down to my chest. She didn't say a word to me. Not a single word. But she smiled and I knew. I knew it right then. Her smile carried more power and delivered more information than a thousand books. I knew that from then on my life would be different. But I took her sister on the date anyway and even took her on a few more dates until I confessed I wanted to date your grandmother instead. The first time I kissed your grandmother, I called her by her sister's name," he says, laughing at the memory.

"She was fuming. Wow was she mad, but I didn't let that stop me," he says. "Tiger, all I know is I have never seen you talk about someone like you do about her. When you know, you know, it's as simple as that. Don't try to think your way out of this. Don't try to rationalize chemistry. Sometimes love isn't served up with the circumstances all perfect. Many times love doesn't come on a silver platter. You gotta mold and change and work with what you got."

"Gramps, I can't afford a trip to Spain to go find her anyway, so what's the point. She might not even be there right now," I say in protest. "This is a fool's quest."

"Too late," he says.

"What do you mean, too late?"

"I bought you a ticket. You leave in three weeks," he says looking practically giddy. "You are going to be happy, even if you are too chicken shit to do it yourself." He slams his palm down on the wooden table and, again, the pancakes, forks, and syrup jump into the air.

"What?" I reply. "Gramps, you don't even have the internet. How could you even begin to buy a ticket?"

"I called Janice," he says.

"Who in the hell is Janice?"

"My travel agent," he says. "She booked my last trip with your grandmother."

"Hawaii?" I say. "That was like 10 years ago. Do travel agents still exist?"

"I guess they do. The ticket will arrive in the mail, at your rat's nest of an apartment in Denver, in about a week," he says. "It's a one way ticket with an open ended return."

My head is spinning. How could I possibly leave now, when Gramps might have Alzheimer's or dementia or who knows what. What about my job? I don't have any money. I feel guilty about leaving him here alone. I feel guilty about the sweetness and kindness of Gramps who just spent six months' worth of grocery money on a ticket for me to go find love. My face is flush and warm.

"What about my job and apartment?" I say. "It's too much money, Gramps. I can't take it."

"You hate your job, Tiger," he says.

My eyes begin to water. I wipe them quickly and am surprised my throat is catching and won't allow me to speak without tears. Finally, I manage. "What about you?"

"I will be fine," he replies, so softly I have to lean towards him to hear. "Yesterday I know I got confused. But I will be fine. You have to go. You need a fresh start. You hate your job, you are single, your best friends are a homeless guy that lives under your stairs and an elderly man who lives in a cabin. Do this for me. I thought you would be excited."

I take a deep breath, look back out the window over the ghost town, past Joe Peanut's grave, and stare at the mountains. Gramps takes on a stern fatherly tone.

"I don't want you here right now. I really don't. You shouldn't see me in any bad ... . Well, there is nothing to worry about, but I just don't want you here right now," he says.

It is a strange feeling, getting an amazing gift from someone whom I know can't afford it. A sacrifice that imbues the act with kindness and love. Gramps has given me the shirt off his back, in his time of greatest need, but it isn't like him to spend so much money.

"Gramps, I'm excited, I really am. This is the nicest thing anybody has ever done for me, but I just don't think, logistically —" He interrupts me, yelling this time.

"You have to get out of here. Before ... ." his fists tighten so hard that blue veins bulge against the surface of his skin. "Don't make me talk about it. I don't want to talk about it. Just do me a favor and get out of the country for a while. I don't want you around right now, do you understand me? Can you get that through your thick skull?"

Gramps stares out the big window. His eyes are misty, but his mouth is firm.

"Look, you have to go find it. Maybe not her but at the very least *it*. You haven't been happy, truly happy since that damned day. I remember you, Atlas, as a boy. You were a bubble of joy. You believed in all possibilities. You believed in magic. You believed in love. Then that day, you stopped. You have to get that back. You simply must," he says.

I stare into my cup of coffee.

"You have stopped following, well, following anything that makes you curious. You are just kind of going through the motions. You gotta take a risk sometimes," he says. "When was the last time you even felt nervous?"

I think about this for a few minutes. I can't recall feeling nervous; I was worried about Gramps of course, but not nervous. I shake my head.

"Exactly. Does going to Spain make you nervous?" he asks.

"Of course it does," I reply.

"Did workin' for your dope Uncle Charlie make you nervous?" he asks.

"No. It made me bored."

"Does opening your own coffee shop make you nervous?"

"It makes me want to puke," I say, smiling.

"How 'bout actually having to speak to your lady friend again when you find her?"

"*If,* I find her. *If* I do, I will probably say something terribly stupid," I say, shaking my head, and laugh.

"Good," Gramps says. "You won't find your stride again until you do something that makes you scared. You can do that or all of a sudden, 40 years will pass, and you will say to yourself, oops, I forgot to start living. Then you will drop dead and nobody will care."

I nod my head.

"Ok, Ok. I get it. I'm going to go to Spain. I'm going to find her." I pause and grab Gramps's old wrinkled hand as he reaches for the maple syrup. "Thank you. Really." I manage to say.

He squeezes my hand, his grip firm, warm and full of life. "You're welcome. Now you just have to go find her, AG."

CHAPTER NINE

$146.15.

I stare at the numbers. They mock me and my very being. I look again, hoping they magically change.

$146.15. This is my bank account balance. My net worth after rent, food, heating, water, and Gramps's jail time fine. I now have $146.15 to my name, and I leave for Spain in three days to track down Isabel.

There have been no more incidents of confusion with Gramps over the past few weeks. I even had Sarah, the officer who arrested Gramps, drive out to check in on him unannounced. She reported that he was not happy to see her, but the house looked to be in order and he was as sharp as a tack. He certainly remembered Sarah and glared at her accordingly.

I need money, but I have no idea where the extra cash will come from. I only plan on being gone for a few weeks, but I can't put everything on credit cards that I will never be able to pay back.

I must admit I am excited at the idea of traveling to a country I have never been to, so I can track down a girl. I feel like James Bond, or at the very least, some sort of renegade.

At the same time, I feel equally, certifiably, insane. My only clues are some circled maps and doodles in a guidebook. I do have a few phone numbers, but I won't know what to say when I call. On top of that, I don't speak Spanish, apart from *hola* and *gracias* and *una cerveza por favor* which I picked up in Colombia.

I have embraced my denial of the very real possibility that Gramps may have a serious condition. I have suppressed the guilty feeling that I should be with him.

Someone knocks on my apartment door. That must be Amanda from work. She told me she has a solution to my money troubles and demanded to come over. I open the door to find no one, only a small tin can on the ground, covered crudely with newspaper and a note attached. I pick it up and look around. There is no one, but the aroma of urine and booze lingers in the hallway. I take the can inside and read the note.

Heya, Atlas, I had a good day today. Some lady gave me $20. I ain't got much, but you told me you was broke too, so here you go. I hope you find her. I am droppin' this off. They will call the police if them do-gooders catch me in the building. By the way I need this can back. You know where I live. - Gary

Inside the tin can, I find a crumpled twenty-dollar bill. Someone else knocks on the door. This must be Amanda.

Amanda thinks this whole Spain idea is the most romantic thing she has possibly ever heard of and has been annoying me ever since. She won't shut up about Spain and the girl. She has taken it upon herself to be my helper, which I have to admit has been nice. I always tend to lean on myself, because, well, I have to. Now it seems the universe is conspiring in my favor.

"Just a minute," I shout. I move a pile of laundry to the floor and kick it under the couch and out of sight. I quickly gather dirty dishes from the coffee table and place them in the sink in the kitchen before opening the door.

"Hey, lover boy," Amanda says as I open the door.

"Oh ... my ... God. Is that him?" a second girl says, stepping into my apartment behind Amanda. Her face is speckled with freckles, and her bright green eyes scan my apartment from behind a few stray locks of curly red hair.

"Atlas, this is Gwen. Gwen, Atlas," Amanda says introducing us. We shake hands.

"This place is sooooo cuuuuute," Gwen squeals, making herself at home. She pokes around in kitchen drawers, walks through the living room into the bathroom and then heads over to the bedroom.

"Hey. Hold on a sec. I didn't have a chance to clean my bedroom this morning," I say.

"Yep. Gross. Underwear on your bed," she calls out from my closet.

"Get out of there please. Seriously?" I say while glaring at Amanda.

"Trust me," Amanda replies.

"This is perfect," she yells from the bedroom. "Oh ... my ... God. My friends are going to be so jelly."

"What is she talking about?" I ask Amanda.

"That's why we are here," she clasps her hands in front of her face. She looks very excited, like she has a secret that she can't wait to share. She is practically bouncing up and down as she explains.

"Gwen is my cousin," she begins. Amanda and I take a seat on the couch.

"I looooove the brick walls," Gwen says as she walks back into the living room and takes a seat.

"So I was talking about you and like, how like, it's amazing that you are flying to Spain to look for a girl," Amanda explains.

"This is like a movie or something," Gwen chimes in. I force myself to smile.

Amanda continues. "Gwen is a sophomore at DU and is looking for a place to rent. She wants to live downtown and well ... you are going to Spain and I thought she could sublet your apartment while you are gone." She quickly claps a few times.

"Boom," Gwen says. She pretends to drop an imaginary microphone on the floor. I feel old.

"But I will probably only be gone for a couple of weeks," I reply. "Then what?"

Amanda takes a serious tone and places her hand on my knee. I don't like strangers touching me, especially 17-year-old girls.

"Atlas, I know you think I'm just a crazy teenager, but I think you are about to like, fall in love, and that takes time. When you find her—"

"*If* I find her," I interrupt. Gwen runs her finger on top of my coffee table forming a line in the dust. She lifts her finger and stares at the gray mark on the end. She looks as though she might be sick.

"*When* you find her, you are going to want to go on some dates, then have like, lots of sex and babies," she says, finally taking her hand off my leg so I can relax.

"*Lots* of sex and babies," Gwen adds. She has a creepy look on her face. I am in my own personal hell. She gets up and goes into the kitchen and opens the fridge. After she is satisfied, she opens the freezer and sticks her head inside to inspect the contents.

"My passport only allows me to stay in Spain for six months, then I have to leave," I explain. "So even if I stay, it won't be longer than that."

"I only want a place for six months. I will add a hundred bucks a month to whatever you are paying now for rent and if you get back early, well we will figure something out," Gwen offers.

"You could stay with your Gramps," Amanda adds.

I must admit this is a good idea. She will pay my rent, and I will make an extra hundred a month on top of that without having to do anything. They both look around the room and back at each other. They are waiting for my response.

"I think you should sell your furniture. Like on Craigslist or something," Gwen says.

"But then you won't have furniture," I say.

"No offense, but this place needs a woman's touch. I will get my own furniture," she replies, while examining my orange couch as if it has offended her in some way.

"So. I told you I had an idea," Amanda says very proudly.

This does solve my problem and selling my furniture would help me raise some much-needed funds. I rub my fingers through my beard, while crunching the numbers and calculating the proposal.

"Oh, and I almost forgot," Amanda reaches into her purse and pulls out an envelope. She hands it to me, and I see my name is written on the front.

"All of us at work, well, we think it's pretty brave what you are doing, and well, we decided to donate our tip jar for the past few weeks to you," she says.

I am touched but immediately feel guilty and uncomfortable. "I can't take this," I say handing it back.

Amanda hands it back to me. "Atlas, you *have* to take it. I know what you are doing for your grandfather and all. Just take it. Let people help you. It makes them happy, too. Please."

My opinion of Amanda has changed in an instant. I certainly don't deserve such an amazing act of kindness. I am getting paid to abandon Gramps.

"It's two hundred and fifty-seven dollars. It's not much, but it should get you some nights at a hostel, maybe a bus ticket or some food over there," she says.

"Thanks, Amanda. This really means a lot," is all I can think of to say. I hold the white envelope awkwardly in my hands.

When my parents died, I was faced with the reality that I would be on my own. I don't have someone to ask for help, no backup plan. This idea of someone helping me solve my problem feels foreign.

"So, it's settled then," Gwen says.

"I guess it is," I smile at them both. We work out the details, keys, and things, then Gwen writes me a check for the first two months of rent.

"Oh, and the homeless guy downstairs. His name is Gary, and he is harmless," I say. "He likes coffee."

Gwen stares at me and frowns. "Gross."

"Well. It's settled then," I say.

They both stand up to leave, and I walk them to the door. Amanda grabs me and gives me a huge hug. Normally I recoil at hugs but after what she has done for me today, I give in. She squeezes tight, forcing the air in my lungs to exhale.

"I'm so excited for you, Atlas," she says. She then whispers in my ear. "And don't worry about Gary. I will bring him coffee."

They both leave, and I'm alone again.

"Holy shit," I whisper.

The guidebook on the coffee table flutters open, stirred by a breeze blowing through an open window. An excitement bubbles up inside of me. This is actually going to happen. I am about to have an epic adventure, and I can't quite believe it.

What if I do find her? What if she actually is happy to see me? What if we do have lots of sex and babies?

I decide to make myself some coffee and get to work listing all of this thrift store furniture online. I pat the top of my prized espresso maker, which would fetch a fine price.

Time to sell my life so I can start a new one.

CHAPTER TEN

"Don't forget to get someone who speaks Spanish to call those numbers in the book. And don't forget to go to the café, the one with the internet password. Oh and—" Gramps barks orders into the phone.

"I know, Gramps, I know," I interrupt. "Don't worry about me. You don't forget to eat. OK? I will be fine."

"You have enough money?" he asks. "I want you to try some of those authentic burritos."

"That is Mexican food, Gramps. I'm going to Spain," I say and laugh as I take my seat at the gate. I double check my ticket and the sign, which is lit up in red above the door: *London,* the first leg of my flight to Spain.

"You sure you are doing OK, Gramps?" I ask.

"I'm fine. I'm fine. Don't worry about me. I'll miss you boy," he says. "Remember. Illegitimi non carborundum."

"Illegitimi non carborundum," I reply.

This is something Gramps always says to me when he gets sad and knows he won't see me for a while. He said it to me when I went on my backpacking trip to South America, and he repeats it again now. It means roughly, don't let the bastards grind you down.

"Good luck," he says.

"Love you, Gramps," I reply into the phone.

"Love you too. I'm proud of you. Bye, Tiger," he says, and we both hang up.

I look around and nervously bite my lower lip. There is a mother and a small child seated directly across from me in the waiting area of the terminal. The child, a little boy, is staring at me. His mom is smiling at him and follows his gaze. "Who's that?" she says in a high voice. "Whooooo's that?" She taps his nose lightly with her finger.

I smile at the little boy, who doesn't avert his stare or smile back. I wonder what he is thinking. Behind the boy is the customer service counter and a man who is yelling at a woman standing behind a gray computer, an employee of the airline, who keeps repeating the same phrase to him over and over again. "Sir, there is nothing I can do."

A constant stream of people flow by in the walkway area, rushing to grab snacks, newspapers, coffee, magazines, gum, books and some sprinting through the masses, panic stricken, hoping to catch their flights. The walkway is a river of humanity and the buzz of muffled conversation is like the sound of fast-moving water. A man peddling credit cards and free airline miles fishes for people as they rush by, trying to get them to stop at his kiosk and bite.

"What the hell," I involuntarily bark, spotting something my eyes can't quite believe. The mother covers her little boy's ears and gives me a look of disapproval.

Uncle Charlie emerges from the stream of people and walks my way. I stare at him in disbelief. He slowly approaches me, and his expression is stern. He is carrying a briefcase and wearing his gray suit as he always does.

"Hello, Atlas," he says as he takes a seat next to me. His lips are pursed and his hands interlaced, resting on his stomach.

"Hi, Uncle Charlie," I reply. "You're the last person on Earth

I would have expected to see today. I didn't even know if you knew I was going to Spain. How did you even find me?"

He simply smiles, meekly and insincerely, looking me in the eyes. He sits up straight and situates himself on the edge of the chair.

"I'm traveling on business, on a layover. I just got off the phone with Gramps. Atlas, I can't let you get on that flight," he says flatly.

I catch a glimpse of the mother sitting across from me. She looks thoroughly entertained and is not even pretending not to listen to our conversation. Her mouth is slightly open, and she looks like her little boy, who is still studying my face.

I shake my head and lock eyes with Uncle Charlie.

"OK. I'm sure you're going to give me a lecture so go for it," I manage to reply.

He attempts to take a kind approach. "When your mom passed I promised myself that I would make sure you were taken care of. No boy should have to lose his parents, and I promised your mom, before she died that if anything ever happened to her I would make sure you were OK. We didn't have the best relationship, your mom and I, but she knew I would never let her down."

"I'm grateful you want to look out for me Uncle Charlie. But this is my life. You're not my dad," I say as coldly as possible. He looks hurt, which makes me feel good. With each word, he is making me more and more emotional, and my right heel begins to involuntarily tap on the floor.

"Look, Atlas, don't you think I know that?" he says. "I know you don't think much of me, but I am successful and relatively happy. That is all I want for you, and getting on this flight is just another way for you to postpone reality. You keep putting off your life to go on these ridiculous quests. You are not getting any younger, and it's time you gave some serious thought to your future."

The mother's jaw is agape as she listens intently. She has given a small plastic toy giraffe to the little boy, and he is gumming it with glee.

"Good afternoon, ladies and gentlemen. We will now begin the boarding process for flight 8435 to London with Group A. Once again, Group A now boarding." The announcement buzzes over the loudspeakers in the terminal.

"Group A to London flight 8435. Now boarding group A as well as all military personnel in uniform, parents with small children, persons that require extra assistance and our gold and platinum frequent flyer members." The woman across from me doesn't budge. Neither do I.

"I'm getting on that flight," I say. Uncle Charlie raises his voice.

"Dammit, Atlas! Your father would not have wanted this for you," he yells as quietly as he can. The vein in his temple is throbbing.

"You don't know anything about my dad," I whisper.

"I knew him longer than you did. I know he was broke when he died. Did you know that? They were about to be evicted from the house you lived in because they couldn't pay the rent with rainbows and butterflies. I know he worried constantly about how to give you the best in life. I know your grandfather does the same. I know they wanted another child but decided not to have one because they couldn't afford it. You don't want to end up like them, Atlas. All of this travel nonsense, and to find out who you are, is all a bunch of crap that will lead you down the path of those who never find contentment in life," he argues.

His words are finding cracks in my way of thinking. They trickle into me, through tiny fissures of insecurity. I fight to follow my heart.

"I can't be happy living your type of life. I can't. I don't want money. That's not what motivates me. I don't want to own lots of expensive things and a huge ridiculous house like you."

"The hell you don't."

"My parents had something, magic—" I say before he interrupts.

"Oh, God. Not that 'magic love' crap she always used to talk about," he says while making air quotes with his fingers. "I love my wife, too, but there is no *magic* about it. We are good for each other. We are a good match. That is reality. There are a thousand people in the world that you could be very content with and love. You need to stop believing in Hollywood's version of love."

I shake my head almost trying to convince myself, more than him. "They were happy. Really happy. I know they were."

"How would *you* know, you were just a boy then, Atlas," he replies.

"Group B now boarding. Group B for London flight 8435." The announcement rings through the waiting area. The woman across from us fiddles with her phone, staring at the screen, now at least pretending not to listen. Her face tells me she has an opinion about love.

"I already tried your way. I did. I gave it a shot. A year. An entire year, and I know I can't be happy in that life, Uncle Charlie. I know you think it's a load of crap, but I want magic in my life again. You don't believe in love because you have a shitty marriage. All I know is that I need to go to Spain because at least there I have a chance to find maybe something more. I don't know if I will, but I do know I have to at least try," I reply, soft enough that the woman sitting across from us leans forward to hear.

"You get on that flight, and I am done," he says. "I mean it, Atlas. Don't come to me for anything. Not a dime. If my life is so bad and my intentions so evil then go, but you have to see I want what is best for you. Can't you see I have experience in the world, more than you, and I might not be completely crazy?"

I take a second before I respond. I know he means well, I do. I can see that, even through my anger.

"But, Uncle Charlie, I'm not you. I have to find my own way, my own purpose," I say. He rolls his eyes.

"The grass is always going to be greener on the other side of the fence, Atlas. Once you land in Spain you will be just as miserable as you are here at home. Why? Because you have no future. There will always be somewhere else. A coffee plantation. A girl. A Spain," he says. "You will never be content. Just like your parents, you will always be coming up with the next wild plan or crazy idea. Never content with what you have."

"Is being content *with* the seeking part, so bad?" I reply.

Uncle Charlie rubs the back of his neck and looks at the floor. "You sound exactly like your mother."

"Now boarding all remaining passengers. All remaining passengers for London flight 8435."

The mother across from us finally manages to tear herself away from our conversation. She gathers her bags and her child and boards the plane.

There is nothing left to say. I stand up and grab my carry-on bag, and Uncle Charlie stands with me.

"I have to go. I'm sorry. I really am," I say and shrug my shoulders.

He shakes his head and looks at the ground, then simply turns around and walks away. He disappears into the stream of people, and then he is gone.

The flight to London is filled to the brim with passengers, outnumbered only by my thoughts, which bounce around in the pressurized air. I can't sleep. I am far too excited, emotionally exhausted, and nervous. I wonder several times if I am having a panic attack. *What the hell am I doing?*

My mind fights to make plans. It always wants to map out my life, which never seems to work out. The more plans I make, the more frustrating life becomes. I am sweating, and Uncle Charlie's words are in my head. I decide to make a list to calm myself down. When I make lists, I know that I am in the middle of a great risk-taking venture.

I release the tray in front of me and grab a notepad, a pen, and the green plastic compass from my carry-on bag. The last big list I made was probably two or three years ago. I realized I had been working at Speedy Coffee for two years. They gave me a small raise to commemorate the event, and I was depressed for two weeks at what a joke my life had turned out to be. I felt old. I felt like I had missed the boat and that it was too late for me to change. I laugh out loud at the thought, which causes the large man next to me to glare over from his computer tablet. He is immersed in some digital book and clearly can't be bothered.

My last big life plan list included things like:

- *open my own coffee shop or roasting company or import sustainable coffee*
- *start saving money and learning how to run a business*
- *find a girlfriend*
- *marry said girlfriend who will be awesome*
- *quit my job*
- *start doing yoga or some sort of exercise*
- *travel*
- *start meditating for at least 5 minutes a day*
- *buy an apartment*
- *try to save some money for a rainy day*
- *ask at least 3 independent coffee shop owners for informational interviews*
- *help out Gary, help him get back on his feet*
- *find Gramps some friends so he isn't so lonely*
- *try to find friends, make an effort, so I am not so lonely*

— *Have kids? Maybe? TBD*

Well at least I will get to check off the travel part of that old list. I have also technically quit my job, even though they promised to employ me again upon my return.

The man to my left, reading his e-book, has won the armrest so I squeeze my elbows into my ribs. The woman to my right breaths heavily, her mouth wide open as drool trickles down her left cheek. Her head keeps falling on my shoulder, and I try to nudge her now and again until she corrects her posture and realizes she is getting cozy with a stranger.

I try to get comfortable in my middle seat and focus on my list. My back and neck have already begun to ache. The magnetic needle of the compass, which I have placed on the tray in front of me, in a spotlight from the reading light above, is slowly spinning. It never stops in any one direction, but reverses course again and again. I write at the top of the page in huge letters.

To Do Next 6 Months
— *explore Spain*
— *find Isabel*

Then what? I tap my pen over and over again on the gray tray. The man to my left looks over at my pen as if to say, *Shut up.*

— *???????????*

Then what? The question marks I write one after another, mock me. They represent a man without a plan. I am terrified. Everyone has plans. Everyone I know is married, has kids, has a mortgage, and a retirement plan. Uncle Charlie would love them all.

I, on the other hand, have a one way ticket to Spain, debt, an envelope filled with tip money from my coworkers, and a crumpled up twenty dollar bill my homeless friend gave *me*, which I hope can last at least a couple of weeks.

"Can I get you something to drink?" a stewardess asks and smiles politely.

"Is it free?" I whisper, leaning towards her as if I am trying to keep a secret. She nods her head yes.

"Orange juice please."

I crumple up my life plan list in frustration and stuff it in the netting on the back of the chair in front of me. I spot an ad on the back of the inflight magazine that reads *Adventure is just bad planning.*

I latch onto the words as if a wise person has written them just for me. Adventure it is. Enough planning for now. I take a deep breath, close my eyes and try to get some sleep.

"Sir. Sir," I wake up to see the woman to my right tapping my arm.

"Sir, we have landed in London," she says and points to the sides of my mouth. I realize I have been drooling and wipe the spit from my face, embarrassed.

The next few hours pass in a jet-lagged blur as I catch my next flight, which takes me to Sevilla, my final destination. When I finally arrive I grab my large blue backpack at baggage claim and catch a bus from the airport towards the city center and my hostel. At least I think the bus is headed to where the hostel should be.

I stare out of the window of the red bus in an exhausted haze. I feel disgusting. A sort of slime has formed on my teeth, my hair is a matted mess, and my beard is greasy. I need a shower, deodorant, and sleep.

All I can see in the darkness are buildings, the soft yellow glow of lights, and occasionally a pedestrian walking along the side of the road. We pass a giant clock that reads 8:00 p.m.

The bus is filled with passengers speaking Spanish, which is the first moment I realize that I am in a foreign country. It invigorates me and sends excitement pulsing through my body.

After about 20 minutes, the bus driver calls out to the passengers. "Plaza de Cuba!"

This is my stop. I grab my backpack and yell "*Gracias*" to the driver, who returns my attempt at Spanish with a look of disdain.

Once off the bus I take in my surroundings. The night air is warm and the streets are filled with people. There is not a blond in sight. I only see dark-haired tan Spaniards enjoying the night. I fit right in. My eyes are drawn to the palm trees that line the streets around me. They are lit up by the glow of the streetlights and make me feel far away from the blue spruce pine trees of Colorado.

I pull out Isabel's guidebook and open to a page Gramps has filled with sticky notes and that contains the map of Triana, the neighborhood where I will be staying. This is where I hope she has decided to rent an apartment and, from her notes, where she has concentrated her search.

I look at the map, then up at the street signs around me until I find *Calle Betis*. I make my way down the cobblestone street and take in a gorgeous night view of a large river, the mighty Rio Guadalquivir, which appears to my right. It must be over 100 yards wide, from shore to shore and is a slow moving liquid giant.

The lights of Sevilla and the Plaza de Toros shimmer on the surface of the dark water as I follow the street, which parallels the side of the river. Pedestrians far outnumber cars as I zigzag past young and old couples out for a stroll.

I walk past dozens of restaurants filled with locals devouring tapas and drinking wine and beer. They spill out of the front restaurant doors, standing outside, gathered around large wine barrels, propped upright into tall, makeshift tables.

I must look ridiculous with my giant backpack and guidebook

as I meander through the well-dressed crowd. The sounds of Spanish fill the air. I hear someone having a conversation in English, at an outdoor table as I walk past, which stands out to my ear in the hum of Spanish like a fire alarm in a forest.

I am looking for the Hostel España, which is supposed to be near here, I think. I finally make it to a bridge that crosses the river and spot another sign, *Puente de Triana.* The side of the bridge is lit by dozens of strategically placed spotlights that illuminate its three gray metal arches, which support the ordinary street above. The arches are just tall enough for a compact ferry to pass underneath, and they are connected by two giant cement anchors that look like massive gray Twinkies half submerged in the river. The bridge is perfectly reflected in the still, slow-moving water below. Ripples form around the cement anchors, the only clue that the water is actually moving. I look at my map and find the Puente de Triana. I am lost. I should have turned left a while ago.

"Can I help you?" I hear a voice struggle with English and look up from my guidebook.

"You can find in map?" he asks. The man is clean-shaven, with spiky gelled dark brown hair, brown stubble on his chin and black eyes. A large gold chain hangs from his neck and the air around him reeks of cheap cologne.

"I'm OK. Gracias," I say, trying to get rid of him.

"Where are you from?" he struggles with the words which sound foreign in his mouth. I can tell he doesn't speak English well. "American?"

"Yes," I reply. "Colorado."

"Like the Grand Canyon." He nods several times, pats me on the shoulder, then gives me a thumbs up.

"No. The state. Not the river," I reply.

"Yes," he says, clearly not understanding. "I love the Grand Canyon. It is very, very big."

I nod politely.

"Where you go?" he asks, pointing to the guidebook.

I tell him the name of my hostel, and he enthusiastically convinces me to follow him. I protest, but he insists. I finally give in and follow him towards the river. We cross over the bridge, which is curious because I don't think we are going in the right direction. I follow him anyway, thinking he knows best.

We hang a right when we have reached the other side of the river and begin a descent down some cement stairs that lead to a pedestrian walkway on the water's edge.

"Are you sure?" I ask.

"Yes, come. Hostel España," he says with a big smile. He leads me under the bridge.

I look around to find we are the only people down here, in the middle of a giant dark shadow of the bridge above. The large full sound of the water hitting the cement columns drowns out all other noise as it echoes off the street above our heads. Despite my fear of being rude, I decide to walk away, but I realize it is too late.

"Give me your money and bag," he says, the grin on his face has turned to evil confidence. He has produced a large knife from somewhere on his body, and he puts it at eye level, about 6 inches from my nose. I can see my own terrified reflection on the surface of the wide metal blade. His English has suddenly improved immensely and I realize what an idiotic mistake I have made. The man looks ready to pounce, as if any loud noise would set him off and cause an instinctive reaction to push the knife into my skull.

Adrenaline pumps through my veins. *How could I have been so stupid?*

"Calm down, man," I say. I move like a sloth. My hands slowly grab the straps of my backpack as I slip them off my shoulders and lower the pack to the ground. I make my motions slow and calm, trying to avoid any sudden movements.

He anxiously looks around and grabs my pack, opening it violently with one hand, all the while pointing the knife at me like a loaded gun. He pulls out my clothes and throws them on the ground. My heart drops as he pulls out the white envelope with my name written on it. He opens the envelope and smiles while pocketing all two hundred and fifty-seven dollars and Gary's crumpled twenty-dollar bill.

"You *are* American," he says.

"Please don't take that," I plead. "It's all I have. My friends gave it to me. Please."

"All Americans are rich." Hatred poisons his words. He quickly rummages through the rest of my bag, throwing the contents on the ground. I watch, completely engulfed by helplessness.

"Your pockets." He points to my jeans. I empty the contents, a pack of gum, my passport, a few euro I had for the bus, and my compass. He grabs the compass, holds it flat and shakes it next to his ear, as if listening for defects. He finally throws it on the ground. He then takes the change, lowers his knife, and sprints off into the dark, leaving me alone.

"Shit. No, no, no, no, NO!" I scream and take a seat on the ground in the middle of my scattered belongings.

I grab my head with both palms and curl up into a ball on the cold cobblestones. The adrenaline rushes out of my body and tears begin to stream down my face.

All of the tension from the day, my life, Uncle Charlie's speech and having a knife shoved in my face releases as I shake, sobbing into a shirt I pick up from the ground. I manage to sit up and blow my nose into the fabric. The salt from my tears coats my lips and beard.

What am I going to do? That money was supposed to pay for my hostel, for food, and keep me going for at least a few weeks. I finally manage to stop crying and look around. There are large trees and cut grass surrounding me on the side of the river. This must be a park of some kind.

I begin to gather my clothes and stuff them back in my pack. I look around again. I want to sleep here in the park to save money, but I am too scared. I have about one hundred and twenty dollars left in my bank account. Time to find the hostel and an ATM. *Illegitimi non carborundum*, I mouth the words to myself. *Illegitimi non carborundum.*

CHAPTER ELEVEN

I woke up early this morning to walk and think about what happened last night. The bright blue sky and early morning sun helps to warm my body and calm my still frayed nerves.

The Plaza De Toros is my first stop as it is just across the river from Triana. I decide to enter the large door in the front of the structure, heading under the painted black letters that label the entrance *TAQUILLAS* and find that the white interior walls are plastered with wonderfully artistic posters advertising bullfights. A large poster in the center of the room captures my attention. It is a replica of a beautiful painting in which a bull, bleeding from its back, has just missed a calm matador, who has lured him past with a bright red cape. At the top big bold black letters declare the location *PLAZA DE TOROS DE SEVILLA*.

"You know why the red cape of the matador is actually red?" An elderly man is standing next to me. I didn't even notice him there. A short sleeve baby blue Polo shirt is tucked into his gray polyester pants, and a straw fedora coolly rests on his head.

"No. I have never been to a bullfight. I don't know. Why is the cape red?" I indulge his question.

"American?" he asks.

"Yes," I say. "And you? Are you from Sevilla?"

"Si, si," he replies. "The matador's cape is red to hide all of the blood."

His English is very good, although he does have a distinct accent.

"If it wasn't red, well, it would get very red during a bullfight," he says matter of factly.

"This bullfight is today." He looks at the poster I have been studying. "You should go," he says.

"I don't know. It's not really something I'm interested in. Not my thing." I politely try to brush him off. I am here to find Isabel and anxious to get started. The thought of watching animals get slaughtered, for fun, does not really sound like a good way to spend my short time here either.

"This is the oldest bullring in Spain," he says. "It is older than me."

"You must be about 40, right?"

He laughs. "Thank you, my friend. I will take that as a compliment. My kids are 40. Here," he hands me a large colorful paper ticket. "You can have my ticket for tomorrow tonight. I love bullfighting and tomorrow are *las novilladas*, which I don't mind not seeing."

"What is *novilladas*?" I ask.

"If you are a matador, and get to fight a bull in this ring, then you know you are a professional. This is where all young bullfighters in Spain want to fight someday. *Novilladas* are bullfights for the bullfighters who are at the bottom of the best. They are not the best yet, but get a chance to fight here in this ring. It is a great honor."

"I couldn't take your ticket," I protest. He has already started to walk away.

"Go, or not, my American friend. The ticket is yours," he yells back. With that, he walks outside and is gone.

I decide to pass through the city center before finding coffee and putting together my search plans for the day. Large horse-drawn carriages, bouncing on the stone streets, clip clop by, full of excited tourists snapping photos. The nostalgic transportation is starkly juxtaposed with a modern red metro train, which slowly carries tourists and locals alike through the center of Sevilla.

I enter the jaw-dropping Plaza del Triunfo and quickly realize why all of today's visitors have flocked here. I simply stand in the middle of the square, my mouth slightly open, unconsciously smiling and examine my surroundings. I have not felt so *in* Spain, so far from home, until this very moment.

To my left is the colossal Cathedral of Sevilla, which is framed by orange trees and taller biblical-looking palm trees. A large watchtower extends to great heights from the far end of the already massive structure, topped by a bronze weather vane which extends even higher from the very top. *You must be able to see all of Sevilla from up there.*

I take a moment to explore the large and lush gardens of the Alcazar, which are a peaceful oasis in the city center. The gardens are huge, as I would expect the late-medieval gardens of a palace to be.

Inside I find a small forest of cypress, lemon and palm trees. Free roaming peacock stroll through mulberries, magnolia, and more orange trees, all enclosed by large castle walls, which protect us from the busy modern world just outside. I overhear a tour guide tell his group that in the spring, when the oranges fall from the trees and start to decompose on the ground, the gardens smell of marmalade.

Back in the square outside, a gypsy woman waves a sprig of rosemary in my face and offers to tell me my future. I am tempted. In truth, there is nothing more I ache for now than to see my future. Before I can resist, she spots the indecision on my face and grabs my hand, leading me to a quiet corner of the busy square.

She is a pear-shaped older woman with dark brown and gray hair drawn back away from her face, gathered in a bun. A long singular eyebrow grows thick above both of her eyes. She is wearing an earth-orange-colored shawl, which covers a simple button up blouse and a black dress that reaches the ground. The woman waves the rosemary in the air around my head and begins to read my palm. Her hands are warm and rough. She smells of fragrant rosemary and sweat.

She traces the lines of my palm with her fingers, up, down, and around as if stirring the cells of my skin for answers. Then she traces the outline of the tattooed compass near my wrist. Her English is bad, but I can understand her.

"You poor, poor boy," she begins. A look of concern furrows her brow.

"What? What is it?" I ask. I don't believe in these things, but I must admit she has piqued my curiosity.

"You have had, em, hard life, yes," she says. "You are lost. You are at a, em, road cross." She closes her eyes, holds my hands together between hers, and squeezes them tight. Then she opens them again, tracing the rosemary over my palm this time. It tickles, which causes me to flinch.

"You take big risk," she says. "Risk good, risk very good."

I smile, then she suddenly frowns, pausing the rosemary on a freckle in my palm. "May beeee, good. May beeee bad. *Depende.*"

"What do you mean? What's wrong?" I ask.

"Very important, you must find path, you path, it is near, but notice signs. Follow signs. No I can't. Yes I can. Yes, you can," she says.

"What does that mean?" I ask. She looks towards the clouds in the sky.

"I see death. Certain death. Someone close to you," she says. I feel a chill fill my body and the hair on the back of my neck stands on end. "But you learn from it. It is new sign, points to path. When you sad, em, sad," she says, making a downcast face. "You on wrong path. When you happy, you on right path. You pay attention and you find home. Home is easy. Sad is hard," she says.

No shit, I think.

She pulls a stick of incense from a brown leather pouch that is tied around her waist and lights the end. The sweet smelling smoke forms miniature aromatic clouds around me as she waves the burning ends over my head, neck, shoulders and legs. I close my eyes, not knowing exactly why. My guess is that she is either completely insane, a cunning business woman, or maybe she actually can see my future. Either way I decide to give in to a bit of wonder no matter how foolish I feel.

She chants something under her breath that I can't quite make out. She then spits in her palm and grabs the lit end of the incense to quickly stop the burning. She holds out the same palm she just spit in, and it is covered with smeared black ash. I quickly understand, as she wears the same look that bellhops do when they want a tip for helping you with your luggage.

"How much?" I ask.

"Six euro," she almost questions, instead of declares. I place the money in her hand. She smiles and quickly pockets the coins. "The thing you looking for is also looking for you," she says. In the same breath she turns and walks away into the crowd, waving her rosemary in the air, searching for her next customer.

I make my way back to Triana and find the small bar that the hostel owner told me about last night. I notice the bull above the bar first. Its large glass eyes are devoid of life. A thick layer of dust rests on its horns and taxidermic face. Its head is huge. I imagine how terrifying it would be to stand in a bullring with this creature sprinting towards you. This particular bull clearly lost its fight.

"Dime," a man behind the bar barks in my direction. I have no idea what that means, but it looks like he is ready to take my order.

"*Dos cafés con leche,*" I say. I am certain I have just murdered the pronunciation. Speaking Spanish makes me incredibly nervous. I studied that very phrase for hours before this trip. I figured I should know how to order a coffee in Spain, at the very least.

The man looks to my left and right. "*Dos?*" He holds up two fingers.

"Oh crap. I'm sorry. *Dos* would be two. I just want one. *Uno*, just *uno*." This guy must think I am a moron.

As the man prepares what will be my first coffee in Spain, I take in the scene.

The bull head is mounted on an elaborate blue and white tiled wall that surrounds the small bar. I would call it a café, but there is a sign that simply states *BAR* on the outside of the building next to the large black wooden door. The bar is on the ground floor of an apartment building that towers above our heads.

Old men pack the room, sipping coffee, and despite the fact that it is 10-o'clock in the morning, some of them are drinking beer. Their conversations are loud, really loud, and as someone new rounds the corner and enters the large double doors that are propped open to let in the sun, people inside shout to greet the newbie. I watch them like an American fly on the wall. They all seem to know each other.

"*Paco. Qué tal?*" a man yells across the room as an overweight bald man, with a white stubble beard and a cane enters.

There are a few kids running around, mothers and fathers in tow. They don't seem to be paying much attention to their children. The kids are sporting miniature suits and brightly colored dresses fit for a doll. Everyone seems to be well dressed in their Sunday best, except for me.

The man behind the bar hands me the coffee, which is served in a small clear glass without a handle, and tells me the price. I am relieved it only costs a single euro. I give him the euro, thankful that I read in the guidebook that you are not supposed to tip in Spain for small things like coffee, at least it isn't as expected as it is back home. I don't feel guilty. I can guarantee I am more broke than him.

I head outside to sit in the morning sun and enjoy the brew. Several metal tables and bistro chairs line the sidewalk and I choose an unoccupied chair and table situated underneath a large palm tree. A small boy practices kicking a soccer ball against a brick wall nearby.

The street is surrounded in all directions by tall, four-or five-story apartment buildings, only broken up by a large cathedral across the street from the bar, which is framed by neatly manicured grass, white flowers, and two large orange trees. The doors of the bar are propped open with two large wine barrels, which several old men are using as a table for their beer and coffee. They read newspapers and watch the activity on the cobblestone street, which seems to be void of cars. The occasional scooter drives by, but most of the traffic is on foot.

I take a sip of my coffee from the hot glass, which warms my hand. "*Café con leche*," I practice the pronunciation aloud to myself. I study the coffee with milk and hold it up to the sunlight like a scientist investigating a beaker.

It is good. It is really good. I take another sip and gaze up at one of the apartment buildings across the street. Laundry hangs outside of most of the windows, pinned to extended miniature clotheslines, waiting for the sun to reach them so that they can dry.

The gentle coo of pigeons, which rest in the bell tower of the church, calms me. I want to talk about last night. I *need* to talk about that asshole thief. But I have decided to tell no one. Gramps would only worry, and telling the police would be a hassle. I just have to watch my spending even more carefully now.

The buzz of caffeine make its way into my veins. It feels good. My brain turns on as if by a hidden switch, and I get to work.

I brush off some dry bird droppings from the top of the black metal table and spread the guidebook out in front of me. I look around the street and scan the people's faces, just in case she might be here. I laugh at myself. Sevilla is a large city, and I don't actually think I will get that lucky on my first full day in Spain.

I grab my pencil and my leather notebook from my daypack and start by writing some notes about the coffee.

Café Con Leche — Spain — Smooth, but strong. Not too milky, creamy, Goldilocks. Just right.

Time to find Isabel. Gramps has divided his small yellow notes throughout the book next to possible apartments. Each note has a phone number and a letter that coincides with the same letter he has written on the map. There are four sticky notes for Sevilla, so four chances for me to catch a break. On the last note, Gramps has written some inspiration for me. I smile as I read it in his messy handwriting, which fills every inch of the small yellow square of paper.

Remember. Even if you don't find what you are looking for, enjoy yourself. Relish in the adventure of it all, Tiger. Remember when I used to hide those purple plastic eggs all over Baldwin? Your parents were trying to turn you into a seeker. Someone who enjoyed the search more than the finding. I used to think that was a bunch of hippie gobbledygook, but I now see they had a point. Remember those treasure hunts as you look for Isabel. I wish I had followed my curiosity more in life. The best people are crazy. And you, my dear boy, you are bat shit crazy. Love — Gramps

A feeling bubbles up in my chest that I haven't felt for a long time. I am excited. I am happy. I am not bored or sad. It feels exquisite and foreign and good. It is as if a fog has lifted from my being. I feel different yet still like myself, like an old friend returned who I didn't know had gone.

I examine the map of Triana. Gramps has circled several

buildings on the map that are very close to where I now sit. I guess I will just go knock on the door of the first circle on the map, because it should be a short two-minute walk from here, and it is conveniently located on the street that leads back to the hostel.

I need to find a phone and someone who speaks Spanish to call these other phone numbers for me. My best shot will be back at the hostel where I feel I might be able to find someone who can help me. If I have no luck with the phone calls, I guess I will simply walk to these other areas on the map as well and see what I can see. Maybe she will walk out some front door, and then she will no doubt panic at the sight of the crazy stalker standing before her.

I pack up the books and start back towards the hostel to begin my search. I head past the cathedral and turn left, looking at my map, up at the street sign, down at the map, then up at the signs again, trying to find the correct building. I slowly walk down a narrow side street until I spot the address I am looking for.

A red bicycle, with a straw basket attached to the handles, leans up against the peach-colored wall of the building. A simple wooden door is propped open next to a large shop window full of wooden guitars, some fully assembled, some almost unrecognizable pieces of wood. The sign above the door is made of carved wood and large letters painted in gold spell *GUITARRERO*. I am confused. This does not look anything like an apartment, and I suddenly doubt Gramps's theory that Isabel is hunting for a place to live. I check the map again just to be sure. There is only one story above the shop, which may be apartments, but I can't see inside of the tall windows above.

An antique metal doorbell chimes when I walk into the cluttered store and the smell of sawdust overtakes me. The shop is full of clamps, guitar strings, large pieces of wood, a wall full of screwdrivers, pliers, hammers, chisels, gauges, cutters, string winders, and guitar body molds. Any available spaces on the walls are filled with pictures of flamenco dancers and guitarists. The store is so full of guitars and tools that I feel if I breathe something will topple to the ground. I examine everything carefully and slowly. I can hear a talented guitar player strumming flamenco music over the speakers in the store.

"*Buenas,*" a balding middle-aged man with perfectly rounded spectacles appears from a corner in the back of the guitar shop. The man is wearing a simple white t-shirt, blue jeans, and a brown leather apron with large pockets in the front. The apron is covered in wood shavings.

"Hello. Yes. Do you speak English?" I ask.

"A little. Yes," he replies.

"Well, I'm looking for a friend and I thought she was going to rent an apartment here." I show him the map in the guidebook. He adjusts his spectacles and examines the page.

"Yes. That is here," he says suspiciously.

"Is there an apartment for rent maybe upstairs?" I ask.

"No. I live upstairs with my family. No rent. We no rent," he explains. He sees the disappointment on my face. "What is your friend's name?"

"Isabel," I say.

"A Spanish name. She is from Spain?" he looks surprised.

"She is yes," I reply. The man smiles.

"She is a girlfriend?"

"Well. Sort of. No. Well I hope so. I'm trying to find her," I try to explain without sounding completely nuts.

"The only reason people visit me is if they are musicians. Guitar players. I make guitars. I make all of them here. I don't remember any girls named Isabel. I am sorry. Are you sure she wants an apartment?" he asks the question I don't want to hear.

"No. It's only a theory. I don't know for sure," I weakly reply and start to head back outside.

"Good luck," the man shouts after me as I leave.

Strike one.

The hostel is located on the ground floor of a five-story building, and I have to use a key to get inside. In the lobby, there is a big couch, and a bookshelf lines the far wall. The bookshelf is filled with guidebooks and novels written in many languages. A handwritten sign, which reads *free book exchange*, hangs beside it.

A tall, curly-haired woman greets me with a giant smile from behind the front desk. Her bright purple-rimmed glasses slip down her nose as she tosses a paper airplane into the room next to the lobby.

A group of young travelers, jamming out to Bob Marley, all chase the paper airplane as it glides past. They are speaking English and look so excited, fresh, and happy to be here.

"Atlas, right?" the woman behind the counter asks.

"Yes, that's right," I smile in return. "What was your name again?"

"Pilar," she replies. "Did you find the café?"

"Yes, thank you. It was really good."

"What are you going to do today?" she asks. Her English is very good but I detect an accent.

I hesitate for a few seconds before deciding to tell her the truth. I tell her about Isabel, about being robbed last night, and about my need for a phone and someone that can call the three numbers I have in my guidebook. After my story I examine Pilar's face, looking for a reaction.

She is amused, *very* amused and enthusiastically replies, "That is awesome. Seriously that is so so sweet." She walks around the front desk and puts her arm around my shoulder, like a big sister. "I am going to help you find this girl. Don't worry, my friend. Come."

Pilar pulls up a second chair behind the front desk and clears a space for us. She picks up the phone connected to the wall.

"Normally we are not supposed to let guests use this phone, but I think you are a special case, Atlas," she says.

"Are you from Spain?" I ask.

"Yes, I am from here in Triana. This neighborhood is where I grew up. I was born here," she says.

"How is your English so good?" I ask.

"I studied abroad in the States," she says. "Now, who do you want me to call first?"

I show her the map and the phone numbers.

"This is a guitar shop, so we can cross that out. You choose," I say.

Pilar closes her eyes and holds her hand above the map. She waves her hand around in the air before bringing her index finger down on the book. It lands closest to the location labeled #3.

"Number three it is," I say.

She picks up the phone and repeats the description of the girl back to me. "Straight shoulder length brown hair, brown eyes, about 5'7", late 20s. Isabel. Right?"

"Yes. Perfect," I reply. My heart rate increases and my palms begin to sweat.

"OK. *Vamos a ver*. Let's call," Pilar says while dialing the number. I stare at her and can't suppress my excitement. I can hear my heartbeat in my ears.

The phone rings, and rings, then Pilar cups her hand over the bottom of the phone. "Voicemail," she says. She leaves a message in Spanish and hangs up the phone.

"Don't worry. They will call me back," she offers some encouragement. "Let's try another."

She grabs the yellow Post-it note marked #2 and dials. After only a brief moment her face lights up, and she gives me a thumbs up.

"*Hola, buenas*," Pilar says. She has a conversation with the person on the other end of the line, and I can't read her expression. Her eyes are squinting and fixated on her left knee.

"Well? What did they say," I ask after she hangs up the phone.

"They do have a room for rent. The woman was very strange

actually. She doesn't remember anyone with the name Isabel. She asked if it was her son's girlfriend. She seemed angry at her son. Like he is in trouble or something. She was very suspicious of me. Anyway, she wants to meet you in person before she tells us anything more," she explains.

"OK. Is the apartment close?" I ask.

"Yes it is. Maybe a five minute walk. No problem," she says. "I would go now. Don't get your hopes up though. She may have more information than she is letting on. She acted like I was a cop or something. I already told her you were on your way. Is that OK?"

"Sure. Yeah," I reply. My search is off to a rough start, but I guess you never know. Pilar gives me directions and I leave my things with her, as I don't anticipate my visit taking very long, and head out the front door of the hostel, carrying only Isabel's guidebook.

I find the building quickly on a particularly worn and haggard looking street. It is almost midday, without a cloud in sight, but the street seems covered with its own invisible shadow. Trash is scattered around and scrawny, starving cats lap water from cracks in the stone walkways. A man, lost in his own head, screams at an imaginary enemy as I try to avoid eye contact. He slowly makes his way past, apparently oblivious to me. If I were Isabel, there would be no way I would choose this apartment.

The door of the apartment building is covered with thick, rusting metal rods, to keep out criminals no doubt. Cartoon music blares from an unseen television through an open window somewhere above. I feel uneasy but buzz the button next to the door, which matches the name Pilar wrote in the guidebook.

A scratchy woman's voice answers and blares through the speaker. "*Que*?" she coughs.

"Yes. Hello. My friend Pilar just called," I explain.

The door buzzes and the latch clicks open. I grab one of the bars, which seems like the iron rod of a prison cell, and cautiously open the door. The stairwell is dark and musty. It smells like garbage and raw sewage. A lazy fly buzzes past my ear. I hike up to the apartment, knock on a red metal door, and wait. I hear a male voice arguing with the woman who answered the buzzer. There must be several locks on the door, and I wait, listening to them slowly unlock one at a time and finally the door swings open.

My heart stops and my eyes bolt wide. I am frozen with fear and instantly enraged. I can't believe it. I *cannot* believe it. Of the thousands of apartments in this city, how? It can't be possible.

The young man who opened the door recognizes me instantly. We both stand at the door, staring at each other. He looks bewildered. I can see him racking his brain with the question, *how did he find me?* He doesn't say a word and then, as if shot from a cannon, he lunges towards me and shoves me backward into the hall, pushing his way past and flies down the stairs. His crimson shirt is a blur of color, and in an instant I can only hear his footsteps in the stairwell.

My head bumps against the concrete wall, but I am able to bounce up quickly, sprinting after him. My instincts fill me with adrenaline and beg me to chase. If I can catch him I just want the money he stole from me last night. I would also feel better if I had the chance to punch him in the face.

I race out the front door of the building and look left, then right. A red blur rushes around a corner, and I follow, running at top speed, chasing him into a narrow side street. I round the corner, ready for anything. I can't get there fast enough and feel like I am running in quicksand.

I bolt into a long alley and see the back of him again, farther from me this time, sprint right, and a car horn blares. The sound of screeching tires cuts through the air, then an angry man's voice shouts words I can't understand. I slow at a palm tree, jog around the corner, and my foot catches on a raised cobblestone in the street. I try to catch myself, but it is too late. My body lunges forward while my feet stay behind, and I crash head first in a whirlwind of dust and street grime.

Suddenly the cartoons I used to watch when I was a kid make sense. When a character was hit with an anvil or a frying pan, stars would float around their head. I swear I see stars now. I am afraid to move. I close my eyes, lying on the ground, and small pricks of white light, stars, fill my vision, barely visible but real enough to me.

My left elbow feels wet. I struggle to catch my breath. I dare to open my eyes and see that a crowd has gathered around me. My elbow is bleeding. The adrenaline pulsing through my body is still numbing any pain.

"*Estás bien?*" a woman lightly touches my shoulder. The sun is behind her, making her face dark. She helps me sit up slowly, tenderly holding my arm as if a gust of wind would cause it to fall off.

The left side of my knee is wet with blood as well, but I seem to be OK. I move each body part, as if testing it out for the first time. My arms work. My legs are not broken. My neck functions properly. My body is shaking.

What kind of fool chases a criminal, on foot, through a city he doesn't know? He could have been leading me back under the bridge, to use his knife again, for all I know. It was a stupid split second decision that I now regret.

About a dozen people stand at a distance from me, pointing, judging me under their breath. I should feel embarrassed, but I am too disappointed to care. The woman helps me to my feet, and I thank her. She looks surprised when English comes out of my mouth. I guess tourists usually don't get this worked up.

I dust myself off and limp back in the direction I came. I don't even bother looking for the young man I was chasing. He is long gone by now.

When I get back to the hostel door, the adrenaline has left my body, and I feel weak in the knees. I start to seriously doubt myself. Maybe the universe is trying to tell me something. Maybe

I should not have come here. For all I know Isabel may not be looking for apartments at all. Maybe the man who robbed me is her boyfriend, and I have terribly misjudged her character. Either way, I only have two more clues to go on here in Sevilla.

The words of Dad and Gramps pop into my head. *Enjoy the search.* Somehow the advice you need makes you feel good, until the very moment you actually need to put it into practice.

"Oh my, wh—what happened to you?" Pilar looks like a panicked parent. I haven't seen a mirror, but I imagine I look pretty bad. My elbow has trickles of blood, dry now, running down my arm, over my compass tattoo, all the way to my wrist. My shirt is covered in dust, and blood has soaked through my pant leg, where it covers the knee.

"You are not going to believe me even if I tell you," I manage to smile at the unlikely and unlucky encounter. I explain to Pilar what happened, and she just stares at me, speechless, in disbelief. Her mouth is half open the whole time. When I have finished my story, she just shakes her head and adjusts her glasses.

"We can call the police," she offers.

"I don't want to waste my time on that. Besides, I have managed not to be killed by him twice now. I don't want to tempt fate. I would also rather focus my energy on finding Isabel. Not on giving police reports and spending anymore time on him," I explain.

"Well, I don't agree. I might call the police when you are long gone from here and tell them the guy robbed *me*. Just to make the world right again," she smiles. "You should get cleaned up. I called the fourth number in your guidebook while you were gone and left another message. There is not much else we can do until they call us back. They will though I promise. I made my messages sound urgent."

"Thank you, Pilar," I reply and head upstairs to shower and

rest. The stress of the day and stubborn jet lag send me into a deep sleep after my shower. When I wake up it is dark outside the hostel. I am confused at first, forgetting where I am. My roommates are back and sleeping snuggly in their bunks. I glance at my phone to check the time. 2:00 a.m.

After what feels like hours of tossing and turning, deep sleep overtakes me again.

CHAPTER TWELVE

"Good morning, sunshine," Pilar smiles and pats me on the back. I feel like I was hit by a truck. I rub my eyes and sit across from her at the front desk of the hostel lobby.

"You went for a shower and never came back. I thought you died, but I am glad to see I was wrong," she jokes.

"Jet lag," is all I can say.

She looks at me and grins. I have no idea what time it is, but it seems early. The only other person in the hostel lobby is a young man wearing a tie-dyed shirt, with long dreadlocks rounded into a beehive shape above his head. He is sitting on the lobby couch, staring at his laptop screen.

"I have some good news for you. While you were sleeping, someone returned my message. It is very good news actually," she says while clasping both of her hands together in front of her face.

"What did they say?" I ask.

"*No me lo puedo creer.* I can't believe this. Atlas, your luck has changed. You may have been robbed, and then I sent you to the robber's house for a visit, but your luck has changed." She is standing now, bouncing up and down.

"What is it? Tell me," I ask, begging her to share. The young man sitting on the couch looks up from his computer.

"The guy who called me back, told me that a girl named Isabel, matching the description you gave me, came to see the apartment he is renting just three days ago," Pilar explains.

"Seriously? What else? Is she here in Sevilla?" I ask.

"He remembered her because she loved the apartment, but when he told her the price she got mad. She told the man that she had been looking for apartments all week, and Sevilla was too expensive. She told him that she was going to Granada. She said Granada was less, *pijo*," Pilar laughs.

"What's *pijo*?" I ask.

"It means, um, in English you would say something like *stuck up*, or what is the word? *Posh*. Yeah, *posh* I think is the best translation," she explains.

"So she is going to Granada," I stand up and start pacing around the lobby like a mad scientist who is on the verge of great discovery. "How? What? I never have good luck." I give Pilar a high five. I am incredibly relieved that Isabel is actually searching for apartments. It makes her seem closer somehow.

"There is more," Pilar continues as if relishing her grand finale.

"What?" I ask.

"I know when she went to Granada," she says.

"How?"

"Isabel made quite the impression on this man, he said she was very feisty. After she insulted Sevilla she asked the man about the bus schedule to Granada, and he gave her a few times he could remember. He distinctly remembers her telling him that she was going to take the earliest bus the next morning. Which means she must have gone to Granada two days ago," she explains.

"She has to be there, right now," I reply.

"You must go to Granada," Pilar says and claps.

"I can't believe this," I say. The dreadlocked young man on the couch is staring at us, curious as to what has happened and why we are so excited this early in the morning.

"You could try to go to Granada today, but I think you need to see Sevilla first. There are two trains tomorrow to Granada, but it will be cheaper for you to take the bus," she explains.

"You can buy your ticket at the bus station tomorrow morning. Trust me. You don't need to book it in advance. But tonight, you must let me take you out into the neighborhood. Let me show you Triana. You should practice how to *tapear*," she says.

"What's *tapear*?" I ask.

"It means to eat tapas. The word is a verb and a sort of Spanish activity. It is an event really. It means you and I will go eat at several different restaurants and bars tonight in Triana. We will eat dinner, not at one place, but several. Enjoying tapas at the bars until we are full," she explains.

"I think you are my new best friend," I joke. "That sounds amazing, but I don't know. I should go to Granada today. Don't you think?"

"Even if you ran out the door right now, by the time you get your tickets and get the next bus, you won't arrive until dark. Take the early bus that leaves at six-o'clock tomorrow morning. She will still be there. I know it. Spanish people are not in a hurry, trust me."

"That makes sense I guess."

"So should I book your bed for tonight, too?" she asks.

"Sure," I reply and reach into my pocket to grab a few euro to pay for my lodging. I pull out the bullfight ticket the old man gave me yesterday and place it on the desk.

"Is that for the bullfight this afternoon?" Pilar asks.

"Yes it is. A random man gave it to me yesterday, but I don't think I want to go. Do you want it?"

"You have to go."

"Why?"

"It's fate," she says.

"I doubt that," I reply.

"When was the last time someone gave you a free ticket to anything?" she asks.

"My grandfather gave me an airplane ticket to come here," I reply.

"He is family, so that doesn't count."

"OK. Well, never then."

"You have to go. Travel is a way to make space in your life for the answers you seek. The answers sometimes come from the experiences that make you uncomfortable and push you in directions you resist. This wasn't part of your plan which means you have to do it."

"Jesus, that's deep."

"Yeah I read it in a book somewhere," she says and laughs. "Just go to the bullfight. If you do I will pay for your room and your dinner tonight."

"You don't have to do that."

"Is it a deal?"

"Well. OK. You have a deal." I can't wait to head to Granada, but I also want the chance to explore during my first trip to Spain.

"Great. Go to the bullfight, and we will go out at nine tonight afterwards," she says.

"For dinner?" I ask.

"Yes. We eat later here in Spain. Come hungry," my new friend says. "I can't bear for you to think of Sevilla as the place you came to get robbed. I want to show you the real Spain. Just don't follow any strangers under any more bridges on your way to the Plaza de Toros."

CHAPTER THIRTEEN

I am nervous. I remember crying the first time I killed a fish, so I may be in for quite a shock. I really don't know what to expect. All I know is, well, nothing really. My opinions of bullfighting come from stereotypes, 10-second clips on the news, and history lessons half listened to.

The atmosphere at the Plaza de Toros is decidedly different from yesterday. This feels like a carnival or even like heading into a ballpark before a baseball game. All of the previously shuttered doors and windows are now open. Colorful flags fly above the main entrance, and vendors selling frozen bottles of water and bags of snacks shout into the air.

There are rows of old men, all dressed like the man who gave me my ticket, sitting on benches in front of the bullring. Some are reading newspapers, some tap their canes on the ground, some are smoking pipes and some simply watch the people walk by. Many of the men seem like they are having vigorous debates, talking with their hands to emphasize important points. I wonder if they are talking about the bullfight and how they think the matador will do.

Once inside the small stadium, I manage to find my seat, or rather a large backless concrete step that acts as a seat. The intense afternoon heat of the Spanish sun beats down on the crowd. Some are waving brightly colored fans, cooling their faces as best they can.

I am only 10 rows or so from the bullring and find this alarming. Blood will flow, and I am going to have a good view. The small stadium is only about half full by the time the action begins, and I settle in for whatever comes my way.

There is a six-person brass band and a large drum propped up in a roped-off section to my left. Trumpets begin to play, and clear notes echo off the unfilled stone seats. The crowd stands to clap and cheer.

I wonder what Gramps would think of all this. I am sure he would love it. Not only the trumpets, but I know he would love the fact that I was trying something out of my element. I know he sent me to Spain to find Isabel, but I am sure he also wants me to get out of my rut and what better way to do that than watch two living things battle to the death.

Just being here and showing up is making me feel like a more courageous person. Somehow leaving home, alone, has boosted my confidence. This is something I did not expect, although I suspect Gramps wouldn't be surprised.

The band erupts into a fanfare; tubas call and the drum signals the entrance of two men riding brown horses. The men are dressed in regal uniforms as if from another time.

They slowly ride their steeds into the center of the bullring, which is perfectly groomed. The dirt is a brownish yellow, surprisingly similar to the yellow of the Spanish flag. The sun casts long shadows of the men who ride around the ring in ceremony.

"This your first bullfight?" says a man sitting to my left. A large camera hangs around his neck, resting atop a fanny pack which is the same shade of red as his sunburned face.

"It is yes," I reply.

"I just got engaged to a Spanish woman. This is my third

bullfight. I'm trying to get to know her culture a bit better," he says.

"You from the States?" I ask.

"Yep. Iowa."

The band begins a new tune, and four men walk out into the ring to the cheer of the crowd.

"Are those the matadors?" I ask.

"No. They are called *toreros*. They are performers, who do participate in the fight, but the kill is reserved for the *matador de toros*, the killer of bulls. That's the matador over there." He points to the opposite side of the ring.

I spot the matador, who is sporting a black hat, which looks like a Mickey Mouse cap with lower-set ears, and an impressive jacket of green and shimmering gold.

After they have walked around the bullring, waving up to us all, the band changes its tune for a third time, and an angry black bull fires out of a gate from the side of the ring. The men quickly scurry behind separate square wooden barriers that are about 4 feet tall and line the edge of the ring every 20 yards or so.

The bull is enraged, as it has been stabbed several times already in the back. He is a wounded gladiator who knows his sole purpose is to seek revenge, to deliver death to anything that moves in the ring. I can almost feel its rage. I also feel it *for* him. The "fight" seems unfair. There are two colorful sticks hooked into his back, and a stream of blood wets his backbone, making it glisten dark crimson in the sun.

The muscles in the bull's chest and back flex as he pauses in the center of the ring. His horns must be the size of my forearm and as deadly as a well-sharpened spear. The acoustics of the bullring are far too good, and I can hear the bull breathing, making him all the more alive to me. I sense his confusion.

He is at the same time angry and confused as he pauses to look around at the people in the stands, no doubt calculating his surroundings, his instincts seeking out the best path for survival.

He seems to stop thinking. I can see him shift to instinct alone as if he knows his purpose.

The dance of death begins. The matador makes his way out into the ring to face the bull. His posture is perfect, and he walks smoothly towards the fiery beast, dangling his red cape at his side. The matador's head is steady. He too knows his purpose, and his focus is precise and sharp. He is making eye contact with the bull.

The bull wastes no time and takes aim for the middle of the matador's red cape. The animal charges the man, who stands his ground, unflinching, and the bull's horn misses flesh by inches. The wind of this charging freight train causes dust to rise around the matador, who spins, finishing with a pose that is both delicate and strong. I didn't notice him holding it before, but the matador has managed to stick another colorful stick into the bull's back. It must be a way of scoring points or part of the sport.

The crowd cheers. They seem pleased. I watch mesmerized by the struggle between two living things that want to kill each other. There seems to be some joy in them both. Two beings locked in a violent dance. The color of the dirt, and the men's costumes, the white paint of the walls, the black-red blood and the blue sky above are by any description beautiful. The path, though, will lead to a terrible end for one of them.

Sweat drips down my nose, and like the bull, I am exhausted by the intensity of it all. I suddenly hate the matador. I look around at the crowd full of strangers, and I hate them all, too. I want the matador to lose. I am tired of false doors, false hope, of always missing my mark. If the bull could only see that his target was not the red cape, but the person standing before him, he would destroy the small man. I know I shouldn't, but I am wishing with all my might, that the bull will stop heading for the decoy, and hit his true mark.

I think of Isabel. I wonder if she is *my* red cape. I know my parents wouldn't think so. But they aren't here in this crowd to tell me for sure. I know Gramps would tell me that my red cape is

Speedy Coffee and jobs with oil companies. Uncle Charlie would be sitting in the front row practically ripping his shirt off with delight at this violence. All the while he would be explaining to me that my red cape is this very trip. He would finish off the bull with a shotgun if he could get away with it.

I can hear the bull breathing fast and steady. My heart rate increases, and my shirt is now soaked with sweat.

"You want some water?" asks the man sitting to my left. "You look like you are about to pass out."

"I'm good, thank you," I reply without taking my eyes off the bull.

The band plays another tune and a blindfolded horse, which is fully dressed in padded yellow armor, is ridden into the bullring as the matador and toreros rest behind the wooden barriers that line the edge of the ring. The man riding the horse is carrying a large, wooden spear tipped with a razor sharp metal end. The bull sees his new target and charges the horse, delivering a blow with its horns into the armor covering the horse's ribs. The brute force of the bull is like a forklift, and his horns lock into the armor and lift the horse's front hooves a few feet into the air.

The man on the horse takes the opportunity to stab the bull in the back several times. The spear goes deep into the flesh. My stomach turns. I hear the bull call out in pain. It is a deep and wild bellow that I not only hear but also feel in a feral part of my soul. The sound makes my skin grow cold, my nerves crawl, and the hair on the back of my neck stands on end.

I want the bull to win with every bone in my body. The men are brave, sure, but this is an incredibly unfair fight. I want to look away, but I can't.

The man on the armored horse leaves the arena, and the matador steps into the middle of the ring. He is now holding a thin, sharp sword, which he steadies firm at his side. He looks like a soldier now. He waves his red cape from side to side, trying to catch the bull's attention and fool him one last time. The black bull is panting and frothing at the mouth, his eyes wild now, dancing with madness. He must sense death.

The bull charges the matador's red cape. Drops of blood make a trail in the dirt in his wake. As he nears the matador, the man raises his sword above his head and at just the right moment, as the bull passes his hip, he thrusts the sword into the bull's neck. But he seems to miss his target, and the sword is pulled from his hand and awkwardly wobbles, sticking out of the back of the bull.

The crowd begins to boo loudly.

"Why are they booing?" I ask the man sitting to my left.

He doesn't look away while he answers. He just leans in my direction so I can better hear him over the crowd. "Well, the matador, if he is good, is supposed to kill the animal in one swift stroke of his sword. He is aiming for a nerve or something in the spinal cord, right between the shoulder blades. If he had hit the right spot, the sword would have still been in his hand and the bull would already be dead. The crowd wants a quick death for the bull. An honorable one. They don't want it to suffer."

"They don't want it to suffer. Seriously? Maybe they should make the fight a little more fair. That matador and all the stabbing make it a little hard for the the bull to win don't you think?" I ask.

"That's the way it goes I guess. The animal has a fighting chance, too. They aren't always this stupid," he replies. His eyes are still glued to the ring.

"What do you mean?"

"If it wasn't so pissed off maybe it would see the matador instead of the cape," he replies.

"But it's unfair," I say.

He shrugs his shoulders.

The sword has finally fallen out of the back of the bull. The matador retrieves it from the ground as the toreros distract the bull away from the matador. He is standing in front of me now, only 10 rows down. I can see him tighten his grip on the sword, and the sweat that is dripping down his face and neck glistens in the sun.

A mix of cheers and uncomfortable boos echo around the ring. A man to my right is standing, shouting, and waving a folded newspaper in his hand. The matador stands firm, unflinching as the bull charges again. At the last minute, the bull gives a flick of its head and its sharp left horn catches the matador's left thigh. To my horror, the end of the horn drills deep into the man's flesh. The crowd gasps in collective disgust.

The bull drives the man into the side of the wooden wall below me. The man is stuck on the end of the bull's horn, helpless to free himself as he calls out in pain. It is the same wild moan the bull made earlier.

The bull picks up the matador with his horn and carries him around the ring. We all watch the man flop around in the air like a rag doll. I feel as if I might vomit, but I still cannot look away. Finally, in the center of the ring, the bull shakes the man again, freeing him.

The toreros rush to lure the bull away from the man and free him, like clowns in a rodeo, so he may live to see another day. You could hear a pin drop in the stadium. The only sounds are of the heavy breathing of the bull, the painful moans of the man, and the other toreros who are yelling to get the bull's attention.

The fallen matador stands with the help of two others, and without thinking puts weight on his injured leg. A gush of ruby-colored blood streams out of the wound, and his face quickly turns white before he falls to the ground. The toreros manage to drag his lifeless body to safety and entice the bull away.

It is wrong, I know, but I feel a sense of justice, balance, and redemption for the bull. The instant karmic play seems right. I wonder, for only a few minutes during the pause, if they will allow the bull to live, since he clearly won. I was mistaken.

Another matador enters the ring. I can hear the sirens of an ambulance just outside of the stadium. The matador and bull repeat the dance. Hooves mingle with bloody dirt, and shoes are caked with dust. The bull charges again, and this time the sword hits its mark. The bull's front feet give way and it falls to the ground, collapsing in a cloud of dust.

The crowd is on its feet now and cheering loudly. The band begins to play as the matador approaches the bull and delivers a final, swift stab of his sword. The bull goes limp. There is no more breathing, only the sounds of trumpets and applause.

I stare at my hands, which are shaking. The man from Iowa nods as I squeeze past making my way towards the exit. It all seems so clear to me now. It is as if a fog is lifting, and I am filled with a new bravery I haven't felt before. The bravery to follow what I know to be true for me and nobody else.

Up until this very moment the anger and guilt I have felt about my parents' disappearance has darkened my path like a self-imposed blindfold.

Life is unfair sometimes. But I can't let the circumstances of my journey blind me. I can choose to see that everything I have always wanted is right in front of me, waiting for me to discover.

I am going to find Isabel. I am going to quit my job at Speedy Coffee and open my own shop.

"This isn't a fool's quest," I whisper, my voice drowned out by the crowd.

CHAPTER FOURTEEN

I take a seat on the big couch in the lobby of the hostel. What an extraordinary day.

"Hola, Atlas," Pilar says as she enters the building. "Sorry I am late. Are you ready?"

"Absolutely. I'm starving. Let's *tapear*," I reply.

Pilar has changed into a white buttoned-up shirt with a large pink peace symbol on the front. Her dark-brown hair is pulled up in a messy bun, and she has switched to bright pink-rimmed glasses.

I catch my reflection in the window as we head out the front door. My dark hair and beard make me look Spanish. Even my skin looks sun-kissed from the day outside. *I fit in here*, I think to myself. That is until I speak.

We walk down the cobblestone street in search of the first tapas bar. Pilar leads the way confidently, and I am lost already as we turn left, then right, then left again, weaving through the dark neighborhood streets of Triana.

"Ah, here we are," Pilar says. "Our first stop."

Las Golondrinas.

The blue and white tiled sign above the door marks our location. I would have walked right past the simple sign if it weren't for Pilar.

As I follow her through the wooden door, the small room, which is filled to the brim with Spaniards, overtakes all of my senses. The smells of fried fish, olives, cheese and an inviting mix of spices fills the thick air. Wine and beer flow easily, spilling from glasses cupped by hands enlivened by passionate conversations.

Pilar elbows her way into the crowd. I notice some people waving at her. A person like her, I am sure, has many friends. A set of stairs to my right leads up to an elevated area where people seated around large tables laugh and dine. Pilar follows my gaze and yells above the noise of the room. "No, no. We stay down here. This is where we tapear. We won't sit down tonight."

Colorful tiles, etched with elaborate designs, line the walls of the room. Each mosaic features the same type of soaring bird.

"This neighborhood, Triana, is famous for ceramics," Pilar explains loudly. "The birds in the tiles here are swallows. That is the name of this tapas bar in Spanish. *Las Golondrinas,* or in English, The Swallows."

We have managed to reach the packed bar, and Pilar waves her hand in the air, successfully attracting the attention of a busy bartender. They both lean closer, ear to ear, tilting their heads so they can hear each other over the loud noise in the room.

After she has ordered, the bartender places two short glasses filled with frothy beer on the bar. Pilar grabs them both and hands one to me.

"Why are they so small?" I ask.

"It's a *caña,* a small beer. We drink these, smaller ones so we can drink all night. Germans drink huge beers because they eat a large meal more quickly. Our dinner will be a journey of sorts, a marathon. There is no need to rush here in Spain. *Salud.*" Pilar clinks her glass against mine.

The bartender slams a small plate piled high with pickled carrots and olives stuffed with blanched almonds on our table. Two thick slices of bread frame the tapa. Despite the simplicity of the food, the flavors pair perfectly with my light Mediterranean-style beer.

"Your first tapa in Spain, my friend," Pilar says loudly. "This place has great food. I have been coming here since I was a little girl. Olives are a staple in Spain. These olives are grown in this area, and they pickle the vegetables here in this bar. It is their own recipe."

We manage to squeeze into a space next to a tall round table in the center of the room. We are elbow-to-elbow with other patrons as we devour robust food and conversation.

"Triana is one of the best neighborhoods in Sevilla," Pilar yells. "At least I think so." She smiles while taking another drink of her beer. Like a breeze, the bartender moves through the room, dropping off a colorful array of morsels at each table. No words are ever exchanged, just empty plates collected and replaced by something new.

"Ahh. The *jamón*," Pilar says. She clasps her hands in front of her face as if a pot of gold has just landed in front of us. The paper-thin slices of dark red meat and white fat marbled throughout look downright sinful.

"This is my favorite," Pilar says. "You must eat this every day before you go back home."

I stuff a thin piece of the cured meat into my mouth, and it melts like a warm piece of butter. I wash it down with beer while expressing my approval. "This is good. It's kind of earthy, salty. Man, that is really good," I yell.

"Do you like it as much as your coffee? I see you scribbling notes about coffee, right? Why are you so obsessed with that stuff?" she asks.

"Coffee to me is amazing because it's so bold and strong. I gravitate towards things that are black and white I guess, and coffee doesn't mess around. It may be strange, but in a messy world that's comforting to me."

"Black and white is boring don't you think? Spanish food is

like a painting. Pair this with that. The flavors are anything but black and white. All coffee tastes the same to me." she says.

She has a point. Spain is like a bucket of colorful paint which has been poured over my head. I am being forced to embrace the vibrant hues. The nuances make me even more attracted to Isabel. If this is where she comes from, then maybe a little color is exactly what I need. If I ever have a chance of believing in magic again, this might just be where I will find it. I am anxious to find her. I can't wait to head to Granada in the morning.

"Pilar! Hola." A woman, who seems to know her, pushes towards us through the crowd. They kiss each other's cheeks before Pilar introduces me. The woman is Pilar's cousin, and she seems to be a little older than we are. Pilar tells her about my quest and reason for visiting Spain. Judging by the look on her face, she doesn't seem to approve.

Pilar heads to the bar to order us another round of beers and the woman, whose name is Rosa, interrogates me. I start to regret the fact that she speaks English.

"You just met this girl, Isabel, once and that was enough to bring you here?" she asks. "I'm sorry, but that is crazy. You probably just want to—how do you Americans put it?—get in her pants."

"No. It's not like that. I promise," I say. Rosa is an intense woman and puts me quickly on the defensive.

"You can't know love unless you get to know someone," she states as if she were an expert on love. "I mean really *know* someone."

"I never said I was in love. Just that I felt an incredible connection with her, and I want to follow that." The words sound crazy when I say them aloud.

"Not to mention there are probably many women you could be happy with. I don't believe in, um, how do you say? Well, in Spanish we say *una media naranja*," she says and scowls at me although I don't know why.

"What is a *media naranja*?" I ask.

"Well. Um. Literally it means half an orange. But you would call it like, um, a soulmate. Yes. I think a soulmate," she explains.

"Are you single or something?" I ask.

"What is that supposed to mean?" she asks and crosses her arms.

"You just seem pretty pissed off that I'm here," I say.

"*Excuse* me? You must think you are pretty romantic, flying across the ocean to find her. I can't help but tell the truth. It is who I am. I guarantee everyone in this bar would tell you that you are crazy, too. You are chasing an illusion. Probably to distract you from your shitty life."

"Like a bull?"

"What? No. Like an *idiota*!"

This would normally cause me to question myself, but the boldness I felt this afternoon has stayed with me. Pilar returns with fresh beers and a new small plate of food. She detects the tension.

"So I am sure Rosa is telling you that love doesn't exist?" She puts her arm around Rosa and laughs. Rosa playfully punches Pilar in the ribs. "She just got divorced, so don't let her tell you love is a scam."

"He flew all this way, Pilar," she argues. "The girl probably already has a boyfriend. He should have hired an expensive hooker instead."

"What is this tapa?" I ask, trying to change the subject.

"Ahh, this is something you cannot find anywhere else in the world," Pilar explains. "This is *ragout de toro de lidia*."

"What does that mean?" I ask.

"It is the meat of the bulls that they kill in the bullfights," she explains with a large grin. I cringe at the thought of my blood-filled afternoon.

Rosa uses another opportunity to pounce. "What is the matter? You don't like bullfights?" she asks.

"I actually went and saw one today."

Rosa raises her eyebrows and cocks her head to the side.

"What did you think?" Pilar asks.

"It was hard to watch. I can't lie," I reply.

"Well. Have you ever eaten a hamburger at a fast food restaurant in America?" Rosa asks.

"Yeah, of course," I say.

"Well those cows have it way worse, let me tell you," she says. "You Americans are crazy. You don't like a beautiful sport because it hurts the animals, then you turn around and get fat from eating tortured cows."

"There is a lot of history around bullfighting here in Spain," Pilar says. "A long time ago, in a village's herd of cattle, there were always overly aggressive bulls, which were called *bravos*. Those bulls were sacrificed in bullfights as a form of public entertainment and, of course, after that the meat was used to feed the town. It was a big party, a *fiesta*, and the poor villages loved this because they rarely got to eat beef. It was both a way to get some meat and some entertainment at the same time. It was a special treat."

"How did the matador do today?" Rosa asks.

"Not too good actually. He was gored through the thigh. It looked pretty bad," I explain.

"Ahhh I think I heard about that on the news!" she exclaims. "Si, si. He almost died because of all the blood he lost, but I think they said he is OK now. Well, he is probably pretty sore, but he is at least going to live."

"I was kind of happy when the bull got some revenge. Is that bad?" I ask.

Neither of them answer. They just look at each other and then down at their beers.

"You saw a pretty bad injury, Atlas." Pilar continues her lesson. "Well historically the bullfighter, if he did well, was awarded the tail of the bull, or maybe an ear, which represented the amount of meat they were entitled to. If the bullfighter killed the bull skillfully, then maybe he would get two ears, which meant he got to keep more of the meat."

Rosa takes a toothpick and samples the tapa, which is smothered in a thick red sauce. "*Carne de lidia*, is meat from the bulls killed in bullfights. There is actually a little market in Triana where all they sell is this kind of beef. It is popular because the meat is actually pretty cheap."

"Go on. Taste it," Rosa demands. I copy her, grabbing a toothpick and take a small bite of the tapa. It of course tastes like beef, but has a more gamey flavor.

"Some say meat carries the emotions and chemicals associated with the emotions of the animal when it was killed," I say, trying to add to the conversation.

"Some say that? You mean vegetarians?" Rosa says. She rolls her eyes.

"Maybe you eat a lot of raging bulls? It makes people cranky when they eat cranky animals," I say while holding eye contact with Rosa.

"There are so many dishes they make with this meat, like bull tail stew and a variety of tapas," Pilar says. I take another bite.

"Well what do you think?" Rosa asks.

"It's good." I shrug my shoulders.

"What's the matter?" she asks.

"I just didn't love how people cheered death. It all felt very barbaric."

Rosa shakes her head.

"But it was also very beautiful. I felt like the matador was truly focused, happy even, and it's a rare thing to see. I also felt like the bull was somehow in his element," I explain.

"The bulls used for bullfighting get to live a pretty good life before the fight if it makes you feel any better. They do suffer the stress of battle, in the end, but before that, as far as a bull's life goes, he has had it as a king would," Pilar says.

"I'm sure they do, I just don't know yet, it was very hard to watch," I say. "I know I will never go to another match again. I wish they didn't have to suffer so much, in the end."

"It isn't really the end that matters, is it?" Rosa says. "It is the life that was lived, is it not?"

Pilar puts her arm around my shoulder. "Besides, think of how satisfying it must have been for that bull, to pierce the man's leg with his horn and then drag him all over the ring. It must have been glorious for him," she says.

We finish our beers, and Pilar says goodbye to Rosa, thank God. "Come. Let's go to the next bar," Pilar says.

I reach for my wallet to pay, and Pilar waves me away. "Please, tonight is my treat. *Te invito*. It's on me," she says. I rub the back of my neck before finally accepting.

We head outside, and I again follow Pilar, this time slightly buzzed, towards our next stop. We round the corner and come upon two men who are singing and clapping, their hands raised above their heads. A woman, dressed in jeans, heels and a teal blouse twirls and moves to the impromptu music. The moonlight acts as their spotlight, and the street is their stage.

"Triana is the birthplace of Flamenco," Pilar whispers. As if on cue, Pilar yells to the trio. "*Olé!*" The two men turn towards us and smile as they continue their song. Their voices bounce off the walls of the apartment buildings surrounding the street. A silver-haired woman watches the performance from her balcony above.

The woman on the street twists and turns and slams her feet violently into the ground, in step and rhythm with the singers' tune. She raises her arms above her head, twirling them around and around like the dancing flames of a fire.

The woman mesmerizes me. The only thing she lacks is the brightly colored flamenco dress I have seen on all of the postcards in this city. I wonder if Isabel dances the same way.

The next few hours are filled with beer, *bacalao*, manchego cheese, tortilla española and *patatas bravas*. We visit an endless array of bars filled with *Sevillanos* enjoying their evenings, as if it were their last here on Earth. I know I will be hungover tomorrow, but I don't care. Tonight I am Spanish and free.

Pilar teaches me about flamenco, how it is like the blues back in the States. The music is a way of expressing pure emotion. It can be happy or sad or angry. She tells me that the singers we saw on the street were singing about how they can't get a job, how the government is corrupt and even though they work hard, they can't pay their bills. "Flamenco is an artistic expression of real life," she says. "The art makes a rough life somehow feel better."

She explains how Triana was once full of Gitanos. The Gitanos gave birth to this type of music. Pilar tells me how in all corners of Spain, Granada, Barcelona, Madrid, Santiago de Compostela, San Sebastian and Cordoba, you can listen to the lyrics of a flamenco song and you will hear them sing of Triana. There is almost always a nod to the music's roots, to Pilar's home.

I like my new friend very much, but I can't wait to leave tomorrow. The possibility of speaking with Isabel, in person, seems real and within my grasp. I will most likely never see Pilar again. I will however, remember this night for a long, long time.

We eventually stumble back to the hostel and enter the lobby, more drunk and slap happy than a few hours ago.

"Oops. I forgot to lock up the computer," Pilar says laughing as she walks behind the front desk. She powers down the laptop and folds it up before placing it in the top drawer of the desk. She then locks it. As she gives the desk one last look before leaving, she spots something that grabs her attention.

"A note for you, Atlas," she says. "Someone called here for you while we were gone, and the front desk person has written you a message."

She hands me a small white pad of paper, and my buzz vanishes in an instant as I read the words.

Message for Atlas Green. From Sarah Piedmont. Please call immediately. Your grandfather is missing.

CHAPTER FIFTEEN

After a sleepless night, I quickly get dressed and head downstairs to check my e-mail. Pilar was able to convince me to go to bed last night, because I wasn't doing anyone any good. She convinced me that I needed rest and a clear head for today. I only agreed after calling Gramps and officer Piedmont about a dozen times.

I am relieved to see I finally have new messages in my inbox. There is a message from the Gunnison County Police Department. I take a deep breath before opening the e-mail and begin to read.

Hi Atlas,

I called yesterday and I hope they were able to give you my message. I see you called several times last night so I assume that they did. My apologies for missing your calls but we were up near your cabin searching for your grandfather, and as you know the service up there can be spotty.

I am happy to report that we did find him.

I exhale an audible sigh of relief.

He is OK, but I am worried about him. Atlas I think he forgot where he lived. We got an angry call from Joe, the landowner where apparently your grandfather fishes illegally. Joe found your grandfather fishing on his land and chased him back to his truck. Joe said your grandfather just sat there, in the truck, for hours. Then he drove away in the wrong direction. The opposite direction from the cabin.

I feel rage boil up inside of me. I need someone to blame for this, and I vow to myself that the first thing I will do when I get back is to drive straight to Joe's house and beat the shit out of him. I will beat him within an inch of his miserable life.

We found him up near Lake Irwin Campground. He was really confused, Atlas. We kept him overnight in the hospital, just to run some tests. You can call him at the number below.
Please call me if you have any questions.
Sarah Piedmont

I sign into Skype after finishing Sarah's message and call the number for the hospital. The phone rings a few times until I hear the voice of Gramps answer the phone.

"Hello," a tired voice answers. He sounds scared and his voice is weak.

"Gramps, it's me," I say. I try to hide the panic in my voice.

A young man sits down across from me in the lobby of the hostel. He has a baby face, short dishwater blond buzz cut hair, and is wearing flannel pajama bottoms and a t-shirt that says, *Beer Me*. He looks like a twelve-year-old college student. I turn away from him and concentrate on my call.

"Who is this?" Gramps says with a hint of annoyance in his voice.

"It's Atlas," I reply. "I heard you were in the hospital. Are you OK?"

"Atlas," he says without the normal smile I usually hear in his voice.

The guy across from me fires up a song on his phone and is playing hip hop through the small phone speakers. I snap at him.

"Hey, do you mind?" I point to my headphones. "I'm on the phone here."

He rolls his eyes and heads into the communal room.

"Gramps, are you OK?" I ask again. He is sniffling and trying not to cry.

"I'm OK," he finally manages to speak.

"I just got a little lost," he says. "But I'm OK now. As soon as they let me go, I can head home."

It is as if every inch of space between myself, here in Spain, and Gramps, a thousand miles away, is filled with awkward tension. I've never heard him distressed before, and it scares me. I don't know what to say so I decide to tell him about the latest developments in my quest.

"I found Isabel. Well I didn't find her exactly, but I have a good lead." I tell him about Pilar and how one of the sticky notes from Gramps led me to my first solid clue. I tell him about the Cathedral of Sevilla, the Alcazar, the bullfight, eating tapas, and the friends we saw dancing flamenco in the street. I wait for his reaction, anything that will ease my worry. Then as if someone had flipped on the light switch to his brain, his voice brightens.

"Well, hot damn, that is good news, Tiger," he says. Strength has returned to his voice. "So you are going to Granada today, right? You have to go today before she moves on or your clue goes cold."

I fight back tears of my own as I recognize in his voice, the Gramps I have always known. I try to act as if I am fine, as if I didn't notice he had slipped from himself before and has now returned.

"What the hell are you doing talking to me on the phone for?" Gramps says. "Go. Go catch a bus to Granada."

"I don't think I should, Gramps. I want to come home," I say. There is silence on the other end. He takes a deep breath before answering. "I don't want you here," he says quietly but with conviction.

"Gramps, you need some help, and I'm going to come home."

"If you come home now, I will never forgive you." His stern voice betrays him and cracks. "Go to Granada first, please."

Gramps used to tell me what to do and I would do it, without a thought. He was the adult, and I was the kid. It also helped that I respected him and loved him with all of my heart.

Go mow the grass over on Joe Peanut's grave. Grab some peanut butter and set the mousetrap. Clean these fish. Have a taste of my beer, but don't tell your Grammy. It was the way my world worked. It was the way I always thought it would be. Gramps knew best.

I reluctantly agree to continue on to Granada, but I don't tell him that I will most likely be coming home after that. He can't push me away. I won't let him. A million questions and concerns bounce around in my head, but all I can say is, "OK, love you, Gramps. Feel better."

"I love you too, Charlie," he says and hangs up the phone.

Guilt fills me to the brim of my soul. *How can I not get on an airplane and fly home right now? Should I? Should I stay here and go to Granada?* I am frozen with indecision.

Maybe I should have stayed home in the first place. I am clearly a terrible grandson. A grandson that leaves his grandfather alone to combat Alzheimer's. And for what? To chase the mirage of a girl.

Alzheimer's disease is a terrible thing. I wouldn't wish it on anyone, especially not on Gramps. It seems to eat away at the essence of who you are, like a maggot on a carcass, slowly working, just below the surface, until that thing that was, no longer is, and becomes unrecognizable.

Gramps is less and less the man I remember. I should want to be there for him, as he becomes helpless with time. I should want to be a comfort to him. I am all that he has. I should leap at the chance to repay him for forming me into the man I am today, for buying me milkshakes at Sweet Pea Ice Cream, for taking me in when my parents died, and for buying me a ticket to Spain so that I might find magic again.

I should, but I don't. There is a reaction in me that I despise. A truth just underneath the surface. The more he slips from himself, I find myself thinking that if he would die, it would be a merciful blessing. I am bitter and scared of what is to come. I resent him for the guilt I feel now. I want to live my life. I want to be free from burden, of being his caretaker. It shouldn't be me. It should be his kids, Mom, or Uncle Charlie. But she is dead and Uncle Charlie is too busy, so the responsibility lies with me.

I imagine Gramps sitting alone now, in the hospital, with a blank stare, lost in his own mind. The thought is pure sorrow, which feels almost tangible. I sense the pressure and responsibility as his caretaker, even though he is thousands of miles away. I am the parent now, of my grandfather, and I resent him for taking my freedom. The freedom that he gave me.

I am a selfish person. I am the kind of person who spends money on chocolate instead of a high quality compass for his parents. There is no denying it now. I resent the man who has given me everything.

The baby-faced young man is now standing in the lobby next to me, barefoot, examining the free books lined up on the shelf in the wall. He is loudly slurping a bowl of cereal and humming to himself.

I decide to try and call officer Piedmont again. I need to talk to someone. The phone rings twice before I hear the tired voice of Sarah on the other end.

"Sarah, it's Atlas," I say.

"Hi, Atlas. Did you get my e-mail?" she asks, her voice is scratchy.

"Yes. I actually just talked to Gramps. Thank you. For everything," I reply. "I actually need some advice. Do you think I should come home?"

She takes a long deep breath before she replies. "I don't know, Atlas. You have to make that decision. The doctors will do some tests today, and I guess if it were me, I would wait to see what they say. You can't make a difficult decision until you have all of the information. I will go over to the hospital today, and I will let you know what I find. OK?"

Her official-sounding voice has taken a human tone. "Don't you have any family you can call for some help?"

"My parents are both dead, Grammy is dead and ..." I pause. I don't want to do it. I swore I would never speak to him again, but I think of Uncle Charlie, who only a few days ago told me that if I got on that airplane, to never contact him again, for anything. I know he meant it, too.

I imagine Uncle Charlie is driving around right now, free as a bird, in a Lexus or some other extravagant car, enjoying his money and his mansion just outside of Houston. Basically, he has done everything right according to society, and I have done everything wrong. He told me that. I just don't think he will do anything to actually help Gramps.

"Atlas? Hello? Are you there?" I stare back at my screen. "Can you hear me?" Sarah asks.

"Yes. Yes, I'm here."

"So you do or you don't have anyone you can call?"

I sigh, then reply. "Yes. There is someone. My Uncle Charlie. I will get in touch with him today."

"OK, good. Well, it's three in the morning here. I'm going to bed," she says.

"Oh, I'm so sorry. I didn't think," I reply feeling foolish.

"It's OK, Atlas. Oh, and I almost forgot. I'm going to send you some links to some helpful articles about Alzheimer's disease. Read them, Atlas, you need to know what you are up against and what is coming. Like I said, don't make any decisions until you have all of the information available to you. Goodnight." The line disconnects.

I close my laptop and look over into the next room. *Beer me* guy has finished his cereal. The bowl is sitting on the floor next to him and he is staring awkwardly at two girls shooting pool in the middle of the lounge. The girls are laughing, and I envy their carefree joy.

Time to shower, write an e-mail to Uncle Charlie, and catch a bus to Granada.

CHAPTER SIXTEEN

Since I only have $65.47 left in my bank account, I check into the cheapest hostel I could find in Granada. It is almost noon, and I don't want to waste any time, so I simply drop off my bag and get to the task at hand, finding Isabel. Coffee is in order. I decide to start with my first clue.

Café Fútbol.

I spot the tattered wooden sign. My guidebook, or rather Isabel's guidebook, has come in handy. This is the place where Isabel wrote the internet password on the small scrap of paper I found in the book. Gramps was the one who noticed the address on the bottom of the paper. Who knows? Maybe I will get lucky and spot her here. At the very least it will be a great place to plan my search.

The café is easy to find, tucked snugly in the corner of Plaza de Mariana, which is filled with tall trees, inhabited at the moment by a large flock of black birds. The small pink- and peach-colored two-story buildings form cozy walls around the square, and the green leaves of the large trees make up a natural dome, only allowing a few small flickers of sunlight to trickle into the square. Gray pigeons peck their way around the stones that line the water fountain in the center of the intimate plaza, and they casually move out of my way as I walk past. A few male pigeons puff up their chests and dance circles around uninterested females.

Patrons, sipping coffee from white mugs and the small clear glasses I've gotten used to here in Spain, pack the outdoor tables of the café. Many people are feasting on long fingers of churros crusted with sugar and piled high on their plates, dipping them in mugs of thick hot chocolate. Elderly men sit on benches that line all sides of the square. Some read newspapers. One rests his hands on his black wooden cane and watches me watch him.

I decide to order at the bar and sip my coffee standing up. Inside, a light layer of sawdust covers the floor of Café Fútbol, and its smell immediately reminds me of Gramps. He always smelled of sawdust after long days in the cellar of the cabin where he formed stumps into beautiful pieces of furniture. Above the bar hangs a large glass chandelier. A waiter, wearing a clean, pressed white dress shirt and a smart black bowtie smiles and asks for my order. I order two coffees instead of just one. The first is a *café con leche* and the second a *cortado*.

I open the guidebook and strategize my plan for the day. I only have two apartments to call and one other to visit, which Isabel circled but did not write the number to. Three chances to find her, I guess, are better than none. I decide to visit each location today in person and then ask someone near each building for assistance.

I finish both of my coffees, grab my notebook, and write some notes.

Café Fútbol — Granada, Spain — 2 Coffees. Café con Leche and Cortado. Both Bitter and burnt. Maybe a reflection of my mood.

The first apartment circled on the map is nearby. It is located where the street Acera del Darro meets a large river called Río

Genil. I pay my bill and make my way out of the plaza, then turn left on the busy Acera del Darro. A giant Corte Inglés towers above me to my left. This American-style department store looks out of place, surrounded by the small mom and pop family bakeries and vegetable shops that line the opposite side of the road.

Mannequins model the latest fashions inside the large sparkling windows of the Corte Inglés. Large automatic doors robotically open as I walk close enough to set off the sensor. A burst of the aroma from a thousand perfumes and air-conditioned oxygen assaults me on the street.

I cross to the opposite side of the busy road, dodging busses, taxis, cars and scooters, before, once safely on the sidewalk, passing a small dusty window of a *panadería*. Freshly baked loaves of bread and sweets are displayed in wooden baskets inside the window of the bakery. Jars of golden honey surround the baskets, and inside a woman wearing a flour dusted apron sells her baked goods to a long queue of customers. The scent of fresh baked bread wafts out of her door, which is propped open. I can't help but slow down as I pass to enjoy the sweet air.

I check my map and turn right onto a narrow street below the tall apartment buildings that populate this area. I keep one eye on the street signs and the other on the buildings above. Many windows have small signs in them that read *SE ALQUILA — For Rent*. There is always a phone number below the sign to call. The first stop circled by Isabel has a phone number written beside it in the guidebook, so I hope to see a sign with a matching number.

The chill in the October air is energizing, and I am filled with a spark of hope. I round another corner and examine the guidebook again. This has got to be the building.

The ugly brick building above me is average in every way. It has no architectural features at all. It is simply a giant brick rectangular building that was clearly built for function, not beauty.

I search the square windows above for rental signs, but I don't spot any. The black metal door in front of the building squeaks open, and an elderly woman slowly makes her way outside. She is pulling a small two-wheeled cart behind her, which looks like a fancy dolly, with a large cloth container strapped to it. I have seen them before, while hitting grocery stores for supplies. This seems to be the chosen means of carrying groceries home in Spain.

"Excuse me?" I say apologetically to the old woman.

She looks at me with skepticism through dark beady eyes. Her hair reminds me of Grammy's, short and curly. She clearly has dyed it, months ago, and long gray roots show under the brownish-red tips of each hair.

"Excuse me. Do you speak English?"

She backs away as I approach her. I get the sense she might be readying herself to smack me. I can empathize with her. If a 6-foot-tall man approached me as I left my apartment, I might be on the defensive, too. I try a large goofy smile to let her know I do not mean to kill her.

Clutching her purse tightly, she elbows her way past me, the squeaky cart in tow.

"I speak English," I hear a woman's voice behind me and turn around. A kind-looking blond woman, dressed in business attire, stands in front of me. "Are you lost?" she asks.

I explain an abbreviated version of my mission, after which the woman seems more than happy to help. She pulls a cell phone from her purse. "Give me the number," she says.

I show her the book, and she dials. Someone answers after only a few rings, and a conversation, in Spanish, ensues. I catch the name Isabel every time my new friend says it, but that is all I understand. I read her facial expressions, which indicate mixed signals. She hangs up.

"The apartment in this building has been rented, but not to anyone named Isabel. Or, at least, the man who answered doesn't think so. He sounded quite excited though and a little, um, eccentric. He wants you to come up," she looks concerned and amused.

"I guess it can't hurt. Maybe he just forgot her name. What is the apartment number?" I ask.

"It is on the top floor, 7C," she replies. "Would you like me to call this other number, too? I have to admit this is very romantic."

"Yes, thank you, if you don't mind," I reply. The woman is pretty enough to make me nervous. She has a British accent, and she smells like flowers. I look down at my feet and stick my hands in my pockets as she dials up phone number two. Another quick conversation ensues and she hangs up and smiles. "The man remembers a girl called asking for the apartment, yesterday, and she is supposed to return tomorrow morning to see it. He didn't get the girl's name, though."

This seems like a legitimate lead. Hope grows within me.

"Well, thank you for your help. You saved me some time. I guess I will have to go and see if it's the right girl."

"You still have one more apartment circled here. You still have a chance with that one, too, right?" she points to the map in the guidebook. "Do you have a phone number for this one?"

"Unfortunately, I don't," I reply.

"Both of these apartments are in the Albayzín. Do you know how to get there?" she asks.

"Sort of. It's where the Mirador de San Nicolas is right?" I ask and point to the area on my map.

"Yes, that's right. Just head that way after you see the man upstairs." She points in the direction of the Albayzín and wishes me luck. I am trying to keep my expectations realistic, but surely, someone at these three places must know Isabel.

The giant brick building towers above, unremarkable in every way. I try to guess how Isabel would judge this place, which of course is foolish as I don't really know her at all. This building needs a facelift. Years of grime and decline from exposure to the elements have left the building looking faded and from another time.

I try the black metal bars of the front door, but it doesn't budge. After a few minutes, a teenage boy jumps down the stairs. When he exits, I catch the door behind him with my foot and let myself in.

There is no elevator in the building, so I clop up the white marble stairs, my footsteps loud and echoing through the cold stairwell. When I reach the top floor and find the door marked 7C, I take a second to catch my breath. I knock.

The door swings open almost immediately, and an older man smiles at me as if I am his long lost son. He grabs me and kisses me on both cheeks, his gray stubble and mustache prickling my skin.

"*Hola, amigo,*" he says while turning around with his hands in the air, dancing what looks like a flamenco jig. He laughs. I can't help but smile. He may be crazy, but his happiness is contagious.

The man's feet are bare and ripped blue jeans, which are covered with tiny colorful droplets of paint, hang loose from his waist. His pants are held up by black suspenders, just like Gramps. A wild matte of gray curls, which seem to be electrified, stick up in all directions on his head.

I look around the large, messy apartment. The air inside smells like paint and fresh air. A few simple pieces of furniture are scattered about the living room resting on a white tile floor. It looks as though they were arranged in the room haphazardly when he moved here, and never settled in their proper places.

A large wooden painting easel stands at the ready in front of two wide doors that open to a balcony outside. Most of the floor under the easel is covered with newspapers to catch droplets of paint. There is a life-size bronze statue of a naked woman standing next to the front door where I entered. She is gazing at the sky wearing only a scarf that covers her arms, which reach for something above.

The man watches me, as my eyes scan the room. The walls are covered with dozens of paintings, so many that I can't tell the color of the walls from which they hang. The paintings are of landscapes, mountains, trees, pigeons, and people. The largest painting of all is of a matador fighting a bull. The painting must be 7-feet tall. It is beautiful. The man's face is delighted as he sees me admiring his work.

"*Ven. Ven,*" he says, taking me by the arm and leading me to the double doors that open to the balcony. He opens them and leads me through.

My mouth drops open at the million-dollar view. It is no wonder I lost my breath walking up those stairs.

"*Río Genil,*" he says pointing down to the streets below which are broken up by a large, winding river. The sun reflects off the current ripples like shimmering jewels. "*Y mira,*" he gestures up and to the left. I follow his pointing finger. "*La Alhambra,* hii hii hiiii," he squeals with delight and does a flamenco jig again turning in a circle and stomping his feet.

The Alhambra, a giant castle, towers above, and makes this a striking view. Swallows fly at eye level, catching bugs, dipping and swirling around us, and the beautiful palace, which is just far enough away to take it all in, glimmers in the sun. People, which look like tiny ants from my vantage point, walk around in the tall watchtower of the castle above.

"*Y mira,*" he grabs my shoulder and coaxes me to look to the right. "*Las Sierra Nevadas.*" The mountains spread out as far as the eye can see, far up beyond the city. The distant dark pine trees give way to fresh snow at the top of the mighty peaks above. I lose myself in the moment and don't notice that the man has left my side until he taps me on the shoulder again and hands me a glass of wine. The glass is filled to the brim. Some wine spills on his paint splattered fingers, and he eagerly licks the wine from them.

"*Salud,*" he says and clings his glass against mine. "I do speak English, you know, I just don't want to." He erupts into howling laughter and I can't help but laugh as well.

"My name is Antonio. Come, sit!" he invites me into the living room and clears some newspapers and painting supplies from a chair, throwing them on the floor.

"Why are you here? I am glad to have you," he says while taking a large swig of the dark red wine.

"Well, I'm looking for a girl named—" he interrupts me.

"*Ay dios mio!*" he looks towards the heavens in ecstasy and closes his eyes. "This wine is good. No. It is great. *Qué bueno!*" In an instant he calms himself and says, "Please, continue."

"I'm looking for a girl. Her name is Isabel, and I think she may have come here, looking to rent an apartment," I explain.

"You look sad. Why are you so sad? I don't trust sad people," he says with a stern face. He takes another large swig of wine, closes his eyes and swishes the liquid in his drooping jowls like mouthwash. I watch him, stunned, as he stands up, walks across the room and kisses his bronze statue on the lips. I try to continue my explanation.

"Well, I don't know, I guess—" he interrupts me again.

"Yes. You. Do. I will ask you again. Why are you so sad?" He sits down beside me, closer this time, on the couch. His wild hair has shifted, to a somehow wilder matte on his head.

"I guess, well, I can't see the future, that's all," I look down at the floor and try the wine. It is actually very good, and I don't know why, but it surprises me. "I guess I've lost something, and I'm here to find it."

The man stares at me for a while and his face slowly lights up. "Don't move please," he commands and quickly grabs a blank canvas and sets it on the easel in front of me. He grabs tubes of paint and a paintbrush and begins to work. I feel self-conscious and uncomfortable as he studies my face.

"So are you renting this place to someone?" I ask.

"I am renting a room. Yes. I need a roommate you see," his brush is moving with passion quickly across the canvas as paint splatters on his shirt and pants.

I think if Isabel met this man, she may have had some serious reservations about living with him. I wouldn't be surprised if he asked her to pose for a nude painting or something when they first met. If they met at all.

"I have rented it to a girl, but her name is not Isabel. Her name is Mariana," he says while he frowns, concentrating on a particular feature of my face.

"Are you sure?" I ask.

"Yes, I am," he says plainly. "You look even more sad than before. Have I clouded your future?"

"I think so, yes. I had hoped maybe you met her at least," I reply.

"Maybe you have the wrong name?" he says while drinking more wine. The glass is almost empty. He walks into a room, past the kitchen and returns with a small painting.

"This is Mariana. My new roommate," he shows me the painting. I am in awe of his talent. The painting is of a beautiful woman with gray hair. She has a large red rose clipped in her locks and large brown eyes, which somehow he has infused with kindness.

"That isn't Isabel. You're right. But I love the painting," I say.

"Do you want to buy it? I will give you a good price. That is why I have to get a roommate. My paintings have not sold well this month," he says while shaking his head.

"I'm afraid I'm broke." I explain my quest in more detail and why I don't have any money. He stares at me with a huge smile.

"Bravo. Bravo. Bravo," he exclaims, breaking into another jig. "You, my friend, have *cajones*." He holds his left palm in front of him, fingers skyward, as if holding an imaginary orange. "You have balls. Balls, my friend. You are an adventure man."

He then lifts his wine glass to his nose and inhales deeply, swirling the wine to invoke its hidden perfumes. He slowly lowers it from his face and keeps his eyes closed while I wait to see what he will do next.

"Love. This wine smells like love," he says before opening his eyes. "It is from *La Rioja*, do you know it?"

"I have heard of it yes. It's in the north of Spain, right?" I encourage an explanation.

"Exactly!" he almost shouts. He sets down the wine and shows me his painting. The rendition of my face. I am blown away and saddened. *Is that what I really look like?* The thought makes me depressed.

He has used dark blues, gray, and dark brown to strike an almost perfect sorrow. He has added water to my eyes, and I am surrounded by blurry streaks of silvery color. He has managed somehow to capture the light of life in my face. The painting is both strange and absolute at the same time.

"So. What do you think?" he asks. He is watching me study his work.

"It's amazing. I look so sad," I say.

"I told you. My paintbrush is a mirror, my friend. It reflects exactly what I see. You are sad because you are not open to life. You think you are separate from life. You *are* life. You are closed off to me. You are closed off to life. Embrace life and you will smile again. Stop fighting against yourself. Stop keeping people at arm's length. Embrace life." He walks over to the bronze statue and kisses her again on the lips. "Come with me," he says.

I glance at my watch. I have already been here for over an hour, and I need to visit two more apartments today. Isabel is not here and I don't have time to waste.

"I really should get going," I say.

"No. Not yet. Come," he won't be swayed so I follow him as he leads me out his front door, back into the stairwell. Instead of down, we head up a separate staircase that leads to the roof of the building. He remains barefoot.

"Are we allowed to go up there?" I ask. He doesn't respond.

He opens a metal door at the top of the stairs that leads to the building's expansive rooftop. I have to shield my eyes until they adjust to the abundant light of day. Rust-colored terracotta tiles cover the roof and several rows of clotheslines, which are full of drying laundry, stretch above them.

The view from up here is even more impressive than from his balcony. We have access to 360 degrees of unobstructed vistas all around. I can even see the center of the city from up here. It feels as if we are in the middle of it all. A soft breeze blows around us as the sounds of car horns and shouting vegetable vendors rise from the city. Antonio leads me to some wooden cages, which are snugly stacked in the farthest corner of the rooftop from the door. As we draw closer I see that the cages are full of pigeons.

"My pigeons." He is delighted. I am confused.

"There are pigeons everywhere in this city. Wild pigeons. Why do you have these in cages?"

"These are special pigeons," he explains. "I have trained them. Did you know that a pigeon can find its way home from almost 950 kilometers away?"

"I didn't know that," I reply.

"It's true. I took this one to Lisbon," he says opening a small latch. He reaches into a cage and retrieves a gray bird. There must be almost a dozen pigeons in the six large cages stacked here. They softly coo as he pulls out his chosen bird. "Yes, this little guy here. I took him to Lisbon, in Portugal, last summer and put a little note in this," he says holding up a tiny brown tube, the size of a film canister.

It has two small elastic straps attached to the top and bottom of the tube. It looks like a small pigeon backpack. He straps it onto the pigeon's back to demonstrate how it works. The sunlight catches the bird's neck and illuminates a thousand small muted emerald-green feathers.

"I let the bird go, in Lisbon, and do you know what happened next?" he asks and smiles from ear to ear. He clearly can't wait to tell me.

"It flew away?" I encourage him.

"Yes. It did. It flew away!" he shouts. A round woman who is hanging her laundry looks over at us with concern. "A few months later I came up here to feed the others, and this one was perched right here. Right here." He points to the top of a wire cage.

"How is that possible?" I ask. He looks pleased that I have asked.

"Because pigeons have very tiny, microscopic pieces of magnetite between their eyes." He places his index finger between his own eyes. "The magnetite is like a small magnet, a natural magnet, that lives in the very cells of the bird. Because of this, the birds can sense the magnetic field of Earth, and this guides them home. No matter where they are, they know how to find home," his voice is quiet now. He whispers, barely loud enough to hear above the buzz of the city. "It is incredible really."

"Wow. My grandfather would love this," I mumble.

"What?"

"Nothing."

"Do you know what I put in the message, on the back of this pigeon?" he asks. I shake my head.

"*A cada pajarillo agrada su nidillo*," he raises his hands to the sky and does his signature flamenco jig as he says the words.

"I don't speak Spanish," I remind him.

"Ah, yes. This means, every bird loves her own nest. You see?" he shouts again. The woman hanging her laundry glares in our direction.

"You know a girl named Isabel is not my new roommate," he says.

"I know. You already told me that," I reply while starting towards the door that leads downstairs.

"She is not my new roommate, but a girl named Isabel did visit me this morning," he says.

I stop moving. "Why in the hell didn't you say that earlier?"

"You Americans are always in such a hurry. I was enjoying my wine. Now is the time," he says and smiles.

"Well what did she say?" I ask.

"She said she didn't want to live with me. I don't know why." He looks down and pets the head of one of his pigeons.

"And? What else?"

"I told her to go watch the sunset up there," he says while pointing up past the *Alhambra* to a hill packed with whitewashed buildings.

"What did she say?"

"She said she was planning on it. If you want to find her I suggest you go watch the sunset, too."

"What's up there?"

"The *Mirador de San Nicolas*. Do you know it?" he asks.

"I read about it in Isabel's guidebook," I reply.

"It will be the best sunset you will ever see in your life. I promise you that much at least," he says. "You look nervous."

"I. Wow. I. Thank you for the information. Thank you," I say.

"You are sad because you haven't found your nest. You will. You will I promise. Now you can go. Go find Isabel. *A cada pajarillo agrada su nidillo.*"

The wild pigeons perched on windows far below scatter to the sound of his voice and fly into the air around us. The sound of their wings echoes off the buildings. I say goodbye to Antonio and head into the city, in search of the Mirador de San Nicolas.

CHAPTER SEVENTEEN

The open square of the Mirador de San Nicolas, which is large enough to fit a small crowd, is situated high in the *Albayzín,* a charming medieval neighborhood of Granada. It is full of students, locals, couples, old people, young people, kids, tourists, and hippies. The dreadlocked hippies have blankets strewn out on the cobblestones around the square. They are hawking homemade bracelets, necklaces, and trinkets while sitting cross-legged on the ground behind their blankets, which are covered with the artist's offerings. Interested tourists haggle with them now and again, but most just admire the trinkets from a safe distance.

Two rough-looking men walk into the square, one carrying a large green glass bottle of beer and the other a guitar. They remind me of my homeless neighbor Gary. Their jeans are ripped, their shirts are dirty, and grime is caked underneath their fingernails. The two men situate themselves at the base of a small tree in the center of the square and begin to play the passionate sounds of flamenco. Between sips of beer, they belt out wonderful music as if to say goodbye to a long lost love, or the setting sun. They seem to be a little drunk, but they sound good. After each song they pass the beer back and forth between them and take long deep swigs.

I scan the crowd. No recognizable faces yet. The same feeling of instant connection I had with Isabel at the coffee shop a few months ago, I sense now, with a city. It feels familiar and foreign at the same time. It is as if I have been here before and that I somehow belong. Above all else, Granada makes me feel profoundly alive.

The view spread out before me is nothing short of spectacular. The Alhambra, Granada's famous palace, is perched atop a large hill in front of us all. From my viewpoint, the valley is steep below me, filled with whitewashed homes, brick-red terracotta roofs, and a maze of narrow stone streets wide enough for people and scooters only. The valley eventually meets a small river that runs through the center of town.

On the other side of the river, the valley rises up again, as if Mother Nature built that hill just for the Alhambra. You could string a very long zip line straight across the valley from the mirador, where I sit, to the palace watchtower and fly above the valley below.

The Alhambra is a massive structure with a tall watchtower at the edge of the hill overlooking the city. The buildings of the palace look as if they are stuck between the Islamic world and Catholic Spain. All of it combined covers what must be the size of two or three city blocks. Most of the grounds are surrounded by fortified castle walls that give way to steep hills filled with giant elm and cypress trees.

The golden-orange rays of the setting sun light up the clay stone walls of the castle, and the snowcapped peaks of the Sierra Nevada Mountains in the distance. The city of Granada is sprawled out below the Alhambra, and I can hear the bells of the large cathedral in the city center and manage to follow the sound until I see the church, nestled in the maze of buildings below.

After a few songs, the two grungy men work the crowd, their guitar extended and turned upside down staged with a few euro on top. I want to give them some money because I truly enjoyed their music, but I can't afford it.

A girl wanders into the square with a group of friends. She looks familiar, and my heart begins to thump. I stand up and cautiously walk towards her only to be disappointed. My ears play tricks on me as well. I swear I hear someone say my name. But over and over again I am wrong.

Swallows dip and swerve through the air feeding on the bugs that the twilight brings. One of the hippies is burning pungent incense that fills the air with spice. An elderly woman, wearing a dress and a flowered scarf over her head, taps me on the shoulder and shows me tuna pastries, which she is keeping warm under a tea towel in a straw basket around her arm. I buy one for my dinner.

I have found a seat on top of the rock wall that connects the square above and a narrow street below. For a moment, I feel calm. I forget about Gramps, my life, and the anxiety of wondering if Uncle Charlie has written me back.

Worry fades with the sun, but disappointment creeps in with each passing minute. If Isabel was going to watch the sunset, surely she would have shown up by now. I watch the colors change on the walls of the Alhambra, from beige to pink to ruby to blood-orange and finally indigo, as the sun leaves the day. The final rays of the sun cut through the air, solid clear yellow, as if we could reach out and grab them.

I study each face in the crowd gathered in the square. I struggle to find anyone who is not experiencing this marvelous scene through the lens of a camera. Some even have their backs facing the palace, trying to get the perfect shot of themselves with this picturesque background. I leave my phone in my pocket. I allowed myself a single photo, but I want to soak this moment up as it happens.

The immaculate gardens of the Alhambra are now lit by moonlight. The city has turned into a sparkling array of twinkling orange lights below me. Granada looks like an enormous and calm lake reflecting the stars above. After the crowd has dispersed and the hippies have collected their wares, I reluctantly decide it is time to go.

It has been a long day, and I am exhausted when I get back to the hostel. All I want to do is crawl into my bed and sleep, but I first need to check on any updates from home.

I grab my phone and login to the network so I can load my e-mails. There are three new messages. I grab a seat in a beanbag. The common area is empty, probably because everyone is out with their friends enjoying the city.

The first message is from Pilar.

Hola, Amigo.
I wanted to make sure you made it to Granada. Good luck and if you don't tell me what happens I will never forgive you.
Saludos,
Pilar

The second e-mail is from Uncle Charlie.

Atlas,
I will be visiting my dad today. Thank you for your concern. I hope you are enjoying your vacation. Must be nice. You should think about coming home if you have a minute. Spain can wait.
Best,
Charlie

Spain can wait? Don't you think I know that? The message is short and to the point, full of jabs. Uncle Charlie knows exactly how to push my buttons. Despite his message souring my mood, I am relieved that he will be visiting Gramps. I am relieved someone else will face this with me, even if it is Uncle Charlie.

The third message scares me the most. It's from Dr. Brown and the subject line reads, *Test Results.* I pause and take a deep breath before opening the e-mail.

Atlas,

I have the test results for your grandfather and your uncle wanted me to send them to you. I am afraid the news is not good. We performed a series of tests, including a MMSI, or Mini-Mental State Exam. Your grandfather got a score of 14. A score of 12 – 30 indicates mild dementia. Twelve or less indicates severe dementia.

We also did a MRI, just to make sure nothing else is wrong and found nothing that would indicate memory loss or confusion.

In my opinion he has Alzheimer's disease. He is in stage 4 or 5, which are the early stages. But it will likely get worse with time.

I am available to talk via Skype this morning. Message me if you are online and I will connect to answer any questions you may have.

Sincerely,
Dr. Brown

I read the words again. Then I read them one more time, as if hoping they will change and the news will somehow get better. Skype indicates that Dr. Brown is online, so I send him a quick message and wait.

Gramps has Alzheimer's, which means he will likely, little by little, forget who I am. The thought terrifies me. I need to get back to Colorado. I feel so close to finding Isabel, but I need to be there for Gramps. If this diagnosis terrifies me, I can only imagine what it must be like for him. He will slowly forget who he is and where in time he is, a stranger in his own world.

My screen lights up. I fumble with my earbuds and quickly answer.

"Dr. Brown?"

"Yes, Atlas? Can you hear me?"

"I can. Yes. Thank you for calling so quickly." I say.

"Of course. You must have received my e-mail. I'm so sorry, Atlas. I'm sure this news is hard to hear. You must have questions. How can I help?"

"Is there a cure?" I need something to cling to, something to give me hope.

"Unfortunately, no. There are drugs and treatments that can slow the disease down and improve his quality of life, but the disease will still win, in the end. There is no cure."

I already have an idea of what Alzheimer's disease does to you, or at least I think I do. I know that it is a type of dementia that affects memory. I feel foolish for not knowing much more. Not only is Gramps forgetting things, and me, but his behavior has changed.

"What is he facing? What's going to happen over the next few months?" I ask.

"The disease progresses slowly, but in the late stages, later on, your grandfather will most likely lose the ability to carry on a conversation. Every time you see him, his memory will always be just a little bit worse, until he doesn't remember anything at all. He will most likely die from this, Atlas. It could be months, or, most likely, years," he says.

I feel a twinge of guilt for not having noticed the symptoms earlier. Perhaps there is something I could have done, to make him see a doctor and perhaps buy him more time. In hindsight, I should have known.

Over the past year, Gramps has started to leave little notes for himself all over the cabin. For example, there is a note on the coffeemaker, with instructions on how many spoonfuls of ground coffee he likes to use for his morning coffee. I even teased Gramps for those notes. It's no wonder he forgot where the cabin is.

"Is he still able to live alone?" I ask. There is a long pause before Dr. Brown answers.

"I understand you are in Spain right now, Atlas. I have a daughter who is studying abroad right now so I understand how hard it would be for her to be torn from that excitement. But to answer your question. He is going to need a caretaker. Maybe not right away, but I would recommend someone lives with him full time. Or you can look into assisted living homes."

"I'm not going to check Gramps into an old folks' home," I whisper.

"Sorry? The connection is weak," he says.

"Nothing. Are there any alternative treatments? Like herbs or something?" I ask.

"No, not really. Those types of things are more for prevention, not treatment. I'm sorry, Atlas I know this is hard to hear. There are clinical trials, though. We can experiment with different drug cocktails and treatments, but they are unlikely to work," he explains.

"Gramps would hate that. All he would want to do, is to be left alone, surrounded by the things he loves. He would want to be at the cabin as much as possible," I say.

"I understand," he replies. "My apologies, but I'm afraid I have to go. If you have more questions please e-mail anytime. OK?"

"OK thanks, Dr. Brown."

I throw my phone across the room. I don't know who or what to blame for this. Life, I guess. Somehow, it doesn't seem fair. Alzheimer's seems like something you should give murderers or criminals as a form of punishment, not the man who has taken care of me for so many years. There is nothing to feed my appetite for hope.

It's my job to make the horrible months and years ahead as bearable as the unbearable can be. Before I can change my mind, I send a quick e-mail to Uncle Charlie.

Uncle Charlie,

I got your e-mail and I just spoke with Dr. Brown. I agree. It's time for me to come home.

I am broke. Can you pay for my ticket?

If you value my being there at this time, please book the ticket for Wednesday from Granada to Denver.

Best,

Atlas

I will have one more day here in Granada. This will be my only chance to find Isabel. If I can't find her by then, I guess it was just not meant to be. Knowing what I know now, I don't think it is a future she would want to be a part of anyway. If I am unsuccessful in my quest, well, lucky her.

CHAPTER EIGHTEEN

Granada is a city that begs you to slow down, so I take my time wandering through her streets, savoring the minute details of her beauty. I have two apartments to visit still, and if fate would choose to intervene, I will find Isabel today. The morning air is brisk and energizes me. I still have hope even if my confidence is fading.

Next to the cathedral, I spot rows of large brown paper bags filled with every spice imaginable. They are all lined up in neat little rows on top of a long dark wooden table, which is shaded by the orange trees above. Bright red smoked paprika, earth-yellow cumin, light brown cinnamon, bark colored cloves, dark red saffron, and a bouquet of smells fills the air, while a busy man sells his spices by the bagful to passersby.

There are covered streets nearby with shops of all kinds selling books, tea, souvenirs, postcards, tiles, and honey from the mountains above Granada. The walls of the buildings surrounding the streets are filled with Arabic words and Islamic art carved into the stone. I have no idea what the words say, but the carvings themselves are beautiful works of art, as if the shape was more important than the meaning. I feel like I have stepped into Morocco.

I make my way to another street, this one also filled with more orange trees and Moroccan tea houses. Hookah pipes and tagines filled with glistening couscous and roasted meat fill the windows I pass. Elaborate rugs spill from shop windows and the smell of incense fills the air.

I cross another street and find myself back in Spain, following the small river below the Alhambra, which towers above to my right, glowing in the morning sun. To my left, the snow-white buildings of the *Albayzín* await me. They are tightly packed together all the way up the steep hill.

Each building of the *Albayzín* is unique. Most have immaculate patios hidden inside their charming walls, packed with lemon and olive trees, and the scent of jasmine escapes from time to time.

I continue to follow my map up the hill despite my legs beginning to burn. The road is steep and my breath becomes short. Sweat starts to drip from my forehead. I am certainly getting my exercise for the day. The road twists and turns through the old white buildings until I turn in the opposite direction from last night, away from the Mirador de San Nicolas, making my way higher.

I check the map again and decide to first go see the apartment of the person who answered the phone yesterday. I walk along the winding streets and finally come to a large white building with a welcoming door.

This large door is less generic than the one I was standing at earlier today. It's made of dark mahogany-colored wood carved with Arabic-looking text. A large artistic sliver of the moon is carved into the place where the door peephole would normally be. If I were Isabel, I would choose this place over the previous generic building, with its cheap black metal doors. It would be an easy choice. This building has character.

I find the corresponding number on the door buzzer and push the button next to the address. It makes an electric buzz, and

I hear it above me as well. The sound comes from an open window two stories up, framed by pink flowers, hanging from a windowsill, which is painted with a blue trim. There is a lemon tree next to the building, full of yellow lemons that contrast with the whitewashed walls. A man answers quickly and he says through the speaker, "*Dime*."

"Yes, um, hello, my friend called yesterday, I'm looking for Isabel, a girl who might rent this apartment," I say into the box.

"*Si*," he replies, and a loud buzz shakes the door, followed by the sound of a lock unlatching. I push on the door, and it swings open.

Once upstairs, a kind middle-aged man with a dark brown mustache and a bald, smooth head invites me inside. Glasses hang around his neck, resting over a dark navy blue sweater. If I had to guess I would say he is an academic.

The apartment is cold, despite the few rays of sunlight that trickle in through the open window. The floor is made of grayish white tile, and the walls are painted an awful, rusty yellow. The apartment is fully furnished, filled with dated wooden furniture, but it does not look lived in. It looks more like a thrift store showroom. There are no family photos anywhere or food on the counters. This all makes perfect sense, I guess, as this apartment is for rent. It smells like lemon-scented chemical cleaner.

"It's cold in here," I say, to fill the uncomfortable silence between us. The man studies me with a quizzical look on his face.

"Come, sit. Here," he says. I breath a sigh of relief. Thankfully he speaks English.

We take a seat on a hideous brick-colored couch, and the man sits down across from me in a small wooden chair. He pulls a short round table between us and grabs a flat, black electric device, plugs it into the wall, and places it under the table. He then drapes a blanket over the top of the table, covers his legs with it, and encourages me to do the same. Our legs are under a sort of tent, with the table acting as the main large tent pole.

"What is that?" I ask the man. Pointing to the table and cord that he just plugged into the wall.

"It is a *brasero*," he says smiling. "A heater. To keep us warm."

I feel the heat under the blanket, and it feels good. The man and I sit around the table like old friends, with blankets covering our legs.

"So you know this girl, Isabel?" he asks. "She should be here soon." He looks at a shiny gold watch on his left wrist. My heart rate increases, and I can hear it beating in my ears. I may have finally found her.

"Well, sort of," I try to explain my situation. I tell him about how I met her and about my search.

"Wow," he says laughing dismissively. "That is quite a story. How many apartments have you visited?"

I have to think about this for a second and pause before responding. "Well, first I was in Sevilla, and—" he interrupts me.

"*No me digas.*"

I don't know what that means, and he tries again in English, seeing I have not registered what he just said. "It's an expression. I am just very surprised. You are really traveling for this girl."

"Yes. Yes, I am. But as I was saying. In Sevilla, I met a friend who called the numbers in my book here, and we eventually got very lucky. We learned she was in Granada."

"There is no luck my friend," he replies.

"I only have three clues, only three apartments in the book here in Granada. I visited the first yesterday, near Café Fútbol." He nods in acknowledgment. "But that apartment has already been rented to a different woman," I say. "I learned she was supposed to watch the sunset at the Mirador de San Nicolas, but she didn't show up last night. So now I'm here."

"Well, if a door does not open, then it is not your door," he says with a sparkle in his eye.

"I guess that's true, yes," I say. "Well *your* door has opened. So hopefully I have found the right place."

"If it is not the girl, then you just have to go find another door," he says softly.

"I actually had a gypsy woman read my future in Sevilla, and she said the thing I'm looking for is also looking for me, so maybe this will be my lucky day," I say.

"Don't pay any attention to those gypsies," he says. "They are no good for Spain. Did you know our government pays them if they send their kids to school? Did you know that?"

"No, I guess I don't know much about them," I say. I hear the door buzzer below, and my eyes bolt wide in an instant, before I realize it was for another apartment. I wipe my palms against my jeans.

"How much did you pay her to read your fortune?" he asks.

"Six euro," I reply.

"*Dios mío.* She would have taken one," he says. "The gypsies, well, they have a long history here in Spain, but now, they get special treatment. They don't believe in school, their kids don't go to school, so they will always be beggars. Do you think the government pays me if I take my kids to school? Of course not."

The door buzzer below sounds again, and this time it is for us. The man smiles. I feel as if I might faint. He gets up and heads to the buzzer box next to the apartment's front door and says, "*Dime.*" A woman's voice responds, and he buzzes her in. I can't quite remember what Isabel's voice sounded like, but it certainly could be her.

I stand up, shedding the blanket, and I can't move. I am frozen to my spot as footsteps echo off the halls of the stairwell. It sounds like she must be wearing heels. The steps get louder, and louder still, until she enters the room. My heart sinks when I see her, and my breath leaves my body.

It isn't Isabel.

"*Hola,*" she says to the man and then notices me standing in the living room.

She is a tall, young woman, wearing a bright teal blouse, a

white scarf, and tight blue jeans. She is wearing light pink heels and dark red lipstick. Her hair is dark brown, and by all accounts, she is gorgeous. The scent of vanilla perfume has accompanied her into the room. But it is not her. It is not her. The man notices the disappointment on my face, and I subtly shake my head as we make eye contact. They exchange some words in Spanish, and she finally addresses me in English.

"You are from England, looking for an apartment, too?" she says. The man has clearly given her a false story. I improvise.

"Um, yes, yes, but I think, I will keep looking, I think you should have it. Um, it's too," the man shoots me a look, his eyes wide and surprised. "It's too big for just me. It's far too beautiful; it's perfect for a beautiful girl like you," I say. She smiles and politely says thank you.

"Well, I should go. Goodbye," I say and shake hands with the man before I leave.

"Good luck with your search. I hope you find what you are looking for," he says and winks.

I take a seat outside on the curb under the large lemon tree to collect my emotions. I am deeply disappointed. I thought I had found her. I realize, at this moment, how badly I want this. I feel my very happiness is at stake. I retrieve my plastic compass from my pocket and open the cheap cracked top to look inside. The red and white metal needle slowly spins, round and round.

The gypsy's words from my fortunetelling in Sevilla play back in my head. *You pay attention and you find home. Home is easy. Sad is hard.* A short-haired gray cat with blue eyes strolls by, eyeing me for food and a scratch. It approaches me and rubs up against my leg, immediately purring with delight. The white buildings that surround the street, along with the lemon tree, block out most of the sun, but the cat leaves me and manages to find a patch of sun to lay in, basking in the warm rays.

I have one more chance, so I might as well get this over with. My hope is fading fast.

I have read about the people that live in caves in the hills above Granada, and I only believe it now that I can see it with my own eyes. As I get higher still, above the *Albazyín* now, the tightly packed white buildings slowly become less frequent and finally give way to steep dirt hills packed with growing weeds, yellow grass, and cactus. The dirt, at its steepest, forms walls which are interrupted by small doors. These doors open into the side of the hills, as if a troll or a hobbit were waiting inside. Some even have small circular shaped windows as well, a few feet from the doors, separated by more dirt.

I curiously peek inside one of the cave dwellings. The home looks normal inside, cozy even. Instead of shingles above their heads, dry dirt keeps out the elements, fortified by the thick weeds and cactus growing above them.

A lavender rocking chair and an old brown dog rest in the shade of a persimmon tree in front of me, which is packed with light orange fruit. The dog stares at me from his spot outside of a cave door, as if I am the strange one. He lifts his head to examine the foreign creature before him. I am the only human in sight. The streets are bare and the only sounds are of the wind blowing past my ears.

I have climbed very high, almost to the top of the hill, and take a second to catch my breath, while taking in a spectacular view. The Alhambra stretches out below me on the opposite side of the valley. I can see the rolling hills that surround the city filled with olive trees, orchards, and small farms. White smoke slowly rises from the fields adjoining some of the farms, perhaps from the farmers burning grass, making way for healthy new growth, of whatever it is they are planning to grow.

There is a slight chill in the air, which has rolled down from the snowcapped peaks of the Sierra Nevadas. I have always thought the air in different countries—cities even—have distinct aromas. I think I could identify where I was, with my eyes closed, just as effectively as differentiating a particular roast of coffee.

Granada smells crisp, with hints of the salty Mediterranean, which is a few hours to the south, and the faintest touch of pine from the mountains above us. A few fig trees line the stone streets in this neighborhood, and I think I may even be able to detect the light scent of fermenting figs, which have fallen on the ground.

The old dog barks at me without much passion before he rests his head back down on his paws.

I open the guidebook to see how close I might be getting to my final clue. I can't locate any street signs up here, only tiles, which are built into the sides of a few scattered buildings, that indicate my location.

I study my surroundings, then the guidebook, then look around again. This has got to be it. The cave house in front of me is the only dwelling anywhere near the circle on my map. My heart rate increases again, just a little bit this time, as I stare back down at the dog, who has found a spot in the sun and has stretched its paws out in all directions. The dog is thoroughly enjoying the warmth of the afternoon October rays.

Hope has taken over my emotions yet again, and I decide the best thing to do is to knock on the door. This door is made of pine-green wood and has the most character of all of the doors I have seen today. The address of the home is at eye level, to the right of the door, spelled out on large white ceramic tiles, in big blue numbers. Colorful, artistic designs filled with tiny purple and yellow flowers border the numbers. On the dirt hill above the door, which I guess would be called the roof, there is a white plaster cone, a chimney, that has a metal chimney cap on top. If you only spotted the chimney cap, it would appear that a house had been buried underneath.

Who knows? Isabel could be inside. The thought sends a bolt of excitement through me. Just in case, I pop a stick of gum in my mouth to both calm my nerves and freshen my breath. If she *is* inside, I want to make sure I make a good second impression.

I quickly rehearse what I will say.

"Hello, Isabel. I don't know if you remember me but ... "

"Hi, Isabel. I was just in the neighborhood ... shit."

"Hola, Isabel. I know this is a little crazy but ... "

Deep breaths. The dog has taken interest in me again. He probably thinks I am a drunk. I walk past the dog towards the door. The dog slowly follows me with his eyes, but doesn't get up or move.

There is a black metal knocker in the middle of the door carved in the shape of a pomegranate. I grab the warm metal and knock twice.

My heart is racing. I haven't been this nervous in years. Well I guess I haven't been this nervous since the last apartment I visited. The footsteps inside approach the door. The latch turns, and the door cracks open just slightly. I can see a short woman who must be in her mid-50s peer through the crack in the door. She looks very suspicious of me and all she says is, "*Si*?"

I stutter. "Hola, hello. Do you speak, um, English?"

"*Inglés*? No. No." She opens the door a little wider, seeming to relax slightly.

Behind her, I can see a tidy home. It smells musty, like the cellar of the cabin, but it is very nice. There is a large wooden table in the center of the room, and a small fireplace. A large leg of *jamón* sits on the kitchen table and a string of white garlic hangs on the wall.

I don't see Isabel. I don't see anyone inside. Disappointment fills me, quickly crushing what was left of my hope.

"Um. Isabel. Do you know Isabel?" I make absurd hand gestures to accompany my words. They are the sort of movements that insane people make when they play a game of charades, just after the nurse has drugged them up.

She understandably looks confused and so does the dog. She is trying, though, and replies, "Isabel? Ahh Isabel. *Una chica como así*?" She plays my game and holds her hand up as if to indicate the height of an imaginary person.

The height looks about right, or at least I think so.

"*Sí. Sí*. Isabel. She was here?" I point down to the ground to indicate our location. "Isabel. Here. *Aquí*." I use one of the only Spanish words I know. She seems to understand and vomits a virtual hailstorm of words I can't begin to comprehend. The only good thing I have gotten from them is that she seems to know something. She slows down and finally realizes I don't have a clue what she is saying. We both stand there, at the door, for a few seconds, trying to think of a way to communicate. I am struck with an idea.

I will record her. I grab my phone and flip on the record audio function. If I can record her, I can find someone later to translate what she is saying. Maybe someone back at the hostel will translate for me.

I demonstrate to her, pointing to my phone. She looks amused and a small smile creeps onto her face. She opens the door completely and motions for me to come inside. The musty smell is stronger inside which mixes with the scent of food. Something simmers in a big pot on the stove, which is perhaps the source of the wonderful aroma.

The woman's hazel eyes are kind. With a big smile, she motions for me to take a seat at her kitchen table. The dog has joined us, and he sits nearby staring at me as if to say, don't do anything stupid or I will have to bite you.

The woman fishes a small knife-like contraption from a drawer and slowly slices thin pieces of *jamón* from the cured, black-hoofed pig leg that seems to be a fixture on her countertop. The leg is nestled in a wooden stand, which must be built for this single purpose. She skillfully places the deep red and white marbled slices of meat in a neat circle on a small plate. She finishes the presentation with a handful of almonds piled in the middle of the slices of *jamón*.

She then sets the plate in the middle of the table and grabs a green bottle of beer from her refrigerator, pops off the top with a metal opener and grabs one for herself. She hands me the ice cold beer, which says *Alhambra Reserva 1925*.

I am overwhelmed by her kindness. She motions for me to eat, and I take a piece of meat and enjoy the delicious Spanish gem. The beer is light and delicious. She sits there and smiles, watching me eat, and sips her beer as well.

I point to the phone again and demonstrate, recording my voice and again call on my very limited Spanish. "*Dónde está* Isabel?" I play back the recording to make sure she understands what I aim to do.

She seems to be on the same page so I push record and repeat. "*Dónde está* Isabel?" I push the phone towards her on the table, encouraging her to begin.

She does and provides a long explanation in Spanish. She points to a guitar next to the fireplace in the small room next to the kitchen. She continues for about a minute before making a motion to signal that she is done. I push stop on the phone. I have it. Now all I have to do is find someone to translate this for me.

The woman's eyes sparkle with curiosity. She must be wondering what some guy, who can't speak Spanish, is doing looking for Isabel. I wonder who she might be. *A landlord, a friend, or maybe family?* Whoever she is, she is kind, and I thank her for that.

We sit in silence for a while longer enjoying the food and beer. Rays of the sun shine through the windows of the cave. Dust particles float in the rays of light and the dog has found its place in the sun again, stretching out as it did before.

The ceiling and walls of the cave house are a sort of carved out white plaster. The ceiling is uneven but looks sturdy enough. It looks as if they dug out this hole in the hill, then plastered the roof and sides with a sort of pure white papier-mâché.

There are framed black and white pictures of some flamenco

dancers hanging on the walls. They look like family photos, not the commercially produced pictures I have seen on the postcards in the tourist shops in Sevilla and Granada. The pictures hang next to large copper ladles and antique-looking spoons.

The woman studies me, following my eyes as I study the room. She begins to talk, then realizes talking is pointless. We finish our snack in silence and I stand up to leave, thanking her for the amazing hospitality.

She nods and pats me on the arm in a caring way. She leads me to the door and waves goodbye as I head back down the hill. The dog stands up and watches me walk away, back in the direction from which I came.

CHAPTER NINETEEN

I focus on directions and navigate down to the center of town, retracing my footsteps from earlier in the day. I can't wait to find out what the woman said, and I quickly march through the city, carelessly bumping into pedestrians, fighting through the crowds, back to my hostel. I need to find someone, anyone, who can tell me what she revealed.

I rush into the lobby of the hostel. There is no one at the front desk, so I head into the common area and am happy to find a handful of travelers hanging out, sitting on the giant beanbags, reading and checking e-mails on their laptops.

"Does anyone here speak English?" I ask no one in particular.

Everyone in the room nods, yes.

"Can anyone translate something from Spanish for me? Just a short recording of audio."

A young dark-haired guy, who is seated on one of the beanbag chairs, stands up and accepts the task. "Yes. I can help you. No problem." He has a British accent but looks Spanish or Italian. "How can I help?" he asks when he reaches me.

I get him up to speed as quickly as I can. "It's a long story, but I just recorded a woman who I need to understand, on my phone. It's very important. I just need you to listen to the message and tell me what she said."

"Sounds easy enough," the young man replies.

We find a quieter corner to stand in, and I forget to ask him his name. I am too preoccupied. I need answers, and I need them fast.

"Ready?" I ask.

"Yep, go ahead."

I push play and watch his face as we both listen to the words tumbling from my small phone speakers. After the recording has finished I beg him to tell me what she said.

"Were you looking for someone?" he asks.

"Yes, a girl named Isabel," I reply.

"OK yes. I understand now. She said she knows Isabel, because Isabel is her niece," he explains indifferently.

"Really?" I can't believe it. I have found a family member. The news is thrilling.

"She said there is no way she will give you Isabel's contact information, though, because she doesn't know you. You may want to harm her niece. She doesn't understand why you are looking for her. I forget the last part, can you play it again?" he asks.

I play it again for him. He looks a bit skeptical of me, too. "She did say that she is in town, Isabel. Isabel is in Granada. In fact she mentioned Isabel likes to eat at *Los Diamantes*."

"What's that?" I ask.

"It's a tapas bar in town," he says. "She finished the recording saying that is all she dare tell a stranger. She mentioned that Isabel might be eating at *Los Diamantes* tonight. She always goes there when she visits Granada."

"So that is everything. Are you sure?" I pry.

He laughs. "She said you seem like a sweet boy."

"Do you know *Los Diamantes*?" I ask.

"Yes, it's where the locals go for tapas; it's a staple here in Granada. It's near Plaza del Carmen."

"You want to come with me? First drink is on me. A thank you for shedding light on my conversation. It really means a lot," I offer.

"I'm very curious about what you are up to, but I have plans tonight," he says. He shakes my hand and offers me good luck before he leaves me alone in the room.

The bar is crowded. People spill out of the doors of *Los Diamantes*. The walls are intricately decorated with blue and white tiles, and the room has standing tables scattered throughout the bar. There are no places to sit here. I think Pilar would approve.

Busy waiters carry small beers to thirsty patrons barking at each other through the noise. The waiters slam heaping plates of fried fish and calamari in front of the hungry Spaniards, who eagerly shove the morsels into their mouths with greasy fingers, chomping on the delicious food with big grins on their faces. Satisfaction is abundant here.

I scan the room looking for Isabel. I don't see her and spot a space, just big enough for one person, to stand in the corner of the room. I squeeze my way into the corner and see a large menu scribbled on a chalkboard behind the bar. The offerings are a dizzying array of fresh seafood from the Mediterranean. I spot a menu on a table next to me as well, and luckily the dishes are translated into English. My mouth begins to water as I read.

Calamares Fritos (Fried Calamari)
Gambas Fritas (Fried Shrimp)
Rape Frito (Fried Monk Fish)
Boquerones (Fried Anchovies)
Boqueroncillos (Fried Baby Anchovies)
Chipirones Fritos (Fried Baby Squid)
Cazon (Dogfish)

Gambas a la Plancha (Grilled Shrimp)
Gambas al Pil-Pil (Chili Shrimp)
Marisco de Motril (Shellfish Motril)
Almejas (Clams)
Arroz (Spanish Rice)
Verduritas Fritas (Fried Vegetables)
Champiñones con Ajos (Mushrooms with Garlic)
Berenjenas (Eggplant)
Tomate Alinado (Marinated Tomatoes)
Pan (Bread)

The bottom of the menu states, *La Tapa es un regalo de la casa, ni se cambia, ni se elige.*

I might as well eat while I wait to see if Isabel shows up. I must look like a creepy loner and am feeling self-conscious. I manage to snag a waiter as he scoops up dirty dishes from a table top near me and ask him about the phrase at the bottom of the menu, "What does this mean? *La Tapa es un regalo?*"

"Em. The tapa is a gift. With purchase of drink. Like all tapas in Granada," he replies.

"Great. One *caña* please." He nods and quickly scurries off to the bar.

I feel completely exposed and embarrassed, standing in a busy bar, completely alone. I pretend to check my phone for messages even though my phone doesn't work without wifi here in Spain.

Finally the waiter returns with my beer and my free tapa. It's a plate of shrimp drenched in olive oil and garlic. The shrimp look as if they were just plucked from the sea. They are whole, complete with heads, long orange antennae, legs and small black eyes. They seem to make eye contact with me, which puts me off a bit, but I go for it anyway. I am not sure how to tackle this type of shrimp so I watch others, who are eating the same tapa near me.

They rip off the shrimp's head, split its hard orange outer shell, then peel it off. The legs seem to be attached to the shell, which is convenient. I imitate the other diners and am pleased with the result. I push the shrimp around in the olive oil and garlic with my fingers before popping it in my mouth. It's fresh and delicious.

I finish the rest of my small beer and catch an elbow in my rib from the person who has squeezed in next to me. A group near me erupts into laughter at a joke I can't understand. Maybe they are laughing at me.

I carefully study the faces in the room, hoping with my entire being to see her. Many dark-haired Spanish women have shown up, but none of them is the *right* dark haired Spanish woman. An hour passes. Then two. I drink and eat an incredible array of tapas fresh from the sea.

It's well past midnight now. I have passed my buzz phase and fallen into full-on drunk. The crowd begins to thin and eventually, I am the last one left in the bar.

I prop myself up, using a standing table to keep me steady. The room is spinning, and my face is warm. The waiter, who has been keeping my glass full all night, sets my bill down on the table.

Isabel didn't come. That's it then. I go home tomorrow. The realization is like a punch to the gut, which knocks the wind out of my lungs.

I lay my head down on the table and let the room spin around me. *My shitty bad luck. My stupid curiosity that led me here.* I hate it all. I hate Alzheimer's disease and my fucking bill, which is far more than I should have spent.

I realize my face is wet. Drunk tears. Damn. I place my money on the table and stumble towards the door. I feel a hand steady my arm. "Isaabellerr?" I slur, looking up, to see the concerned face of the waiter.

"Are you OK?" he asks.

"Yer not Isa. I'm fine," I say and he releases my arm.

I stumble out into the crowded streets of Granada. It must be three in the morning, but you wouldn't know it by how many people are still out enjoying the night.

I kick the wall. I am glad for the pain in my toes and sit on the street propping myself up against the outer wall of *Los Diamantes*, watching carefree friends pass, arm in arm, headed no doubt somewhere fun. I hate them all and their perfect lives.

Suddenly I am sick, and I turn my head to vomit onto the street. My body shakes violently, and I hear a group giggle as they pass. No one stops to help. They all avoid me like I am contagious.

I have failed in my quest. Tomorrow I go home to care for Gramps and figure out my life.

A life without Isabel.

CHAPTER TWENTY

Gramps passed away while I was somewhere over the Atlantic. He died with Uncle Charlie by his side.

I swear I felt it the moment it happened. A profound sadness blew over me, which I brushed aside, thinking it was just my overall mood and my hangover.

They told me he passed away in his sleep. His heart just stopped. Apparently, on top of Alzheimer's, Gramps had caught a bad cold at the hospital, which turned into pneumonia, which led to his death.

I feel only two things: numbness and anger. I watch Uncle Charlie from a distance while I blow warm air into my cold trumpet, trying to warm up the shiny silver Stradivarius, before I play taps. Gramps and I hadn't played the trumpet together for years, but I think it will be something he would love, if he can hear me now, wherever he has gone.

I can't bear small talk with strangers today and sit as far away from everyone as possible, using my trumpet as a sort of excuse. I fiddle with the valves and blow air through it again and again.

It is a cold cloudy Colorado morning. Fall is giving way to winter. I watch the white puffs of breath, exhaled from the handful of people who have shown up for Gramps's funeral.

They are all wearing black overcoats, black dresses, black pants, and black shoes. They match the cemetery and the crows flying above.

The trees are all hibernating for the winter, bare of leaves. The branches are dark and wiry against the gray sky. I couldn't feel more cold, the lifelessness of the day chills me to my soul. He will be buried next to Grammy and his father and mother in the Gunnison Cemetery.

The small group of people must be talking about me as I see their sympathetic faces turn in my direction every now and again. The small crowd makes me sad. Gramps was a good person, an amazing and decent human being. So why isn't this cemetery packed with hundreds of people? I count 12 total, which includes myself, Uncle Charlie, and the preacher.

The preacher takes his place near the grave, and all of us gather round to hear his words of comfort. I can't concentrate on his speech. I just stare at the casket until my name jolts me from a daydream. It is time for taps. My last goodbye to Gramps.

I raise the cold mouthpiece to my lips and begin to play. I surprise myself with an even and clear tone, filling the cemetery. Even the crows grow silent to listen. The tune evokes tears from all present and even Uncle Charlie, who I thought didn't have a heart, begins to cry.

My eyes are dry. I am too numb and too angry for tears. I finish the song and slowly lower the trumpet from my lips. The last notes echo through the air, and my thoughts follow them as they fade into silence. I can almost hear Gramps in my head: *Not bad, Tiger, not bad.*

Someone grabs a shovel and throws the ceremonial first scoops of dirt onto the wooden casket. The preacher says something about ashes and dust. There is no heart in his voice, though, as if he does this all too often, a sad routine.

Everyone makes their way back to waiting cars. I stay, so I can say goodbye to Gramps alone. Just like that, it is all over: the funeral and Gramps's life.

Why did he have to die on a Thursday, while I was flying home? It all seems so pointless. All the while, I was focused on Alzheimer's disease. I was worried about the future and all of the terrible things the disease would bring. I forgot the fact that the future is promised to no one. It seems worrying was a pointless exercise of misguided angst. In the movies, the timing is always better. I should have at least been able to see him one last time. I wanted to thank him for being my grandfather and my substitute dad.

I examine the granite headstone above his grave. I helped Gramps pick it out when Grammy died. It's simple and gray, like the clouds overhead. At the top it says, *GREEN*, in big capital letters. There are two pine trees carved on both sides and in the middle a nice engraved sketch of the cabin. Over the cabin in small letters, I trace the words *Together Forever* with my fingers. The headstone is cold. Grammy's name, date of birth, and death are engraved on the right of the stone and Gramps's will be engraved in the coming days.

"Well, goodbye, Gramps," I say quietly, feeling foolish for speaking to a dead man in a wooden casket.

The casket is made from beetle kill pine. Uncle Charlie and I had an argument over this, too. I insisted on a wooden coffin made from trees here in Colorado. Gramps would have wanted it that way. Uncle Charlie wanted a "proper" coffin, a glossy monstrosity he found online.

I study the grains of wood, which carry waves of blue, the signature stain left from the beetles that killed this tree. I find it comforting somehow. From something so destructive, a beetle that can bring down an entire forest, comes a beautiful piece of wood. That is why Gramps loved to work with this pine. He used it to create beautiful tables, TV stands, cutting boards, and chairs. This wood pleased him most of all. "Beauty from death," he would always say.

I grab Gramps's fly box from my jacket pocket and lay it on a particularly beautiful part of the pine. The pale, colorless day helps highlight the vein of blue in the wood. I retrieve the green plastic compass from my pocket and sit on a mound of dark brown wet dirt next to the grave. I can feel moisture seep through my pants, but I don't care.

"I'm gonna miss you, Gramps." My voice cracks and betrays my previously numb state.

"You are literally all I have ... *I had*," I whisper. The tears, salty and warm, fall easily now.

I open the compass, examining the small crack in the plastic, smiling at the memory of it as the needle slowly spins, as it always has. A profound loneliness envelopes me, thick and dark it covers me, as I study the compass. It reminds me of my parents, of Grammy, and of Gramps. I can't bear to keep it anymore. I carefully place the compass next to the fly box on the pine. It contains too many memories, and the thing I want most in this world, right now, is to forget.

I glance behind me to make sure no one is watching. Most of the cars are driving down the dirt hill, towards the highway. I feel oddly possessive of Gramps, his dead body inside the pine box. I whisper to him, "I didn't find the girl. I didn't find Isabel. I'm sorry I wasn't here ... with you instead. I'm so sorry."

I punch the dark brown dirt next to the ground. I slam my fist down again happy for some physical pain, instead of this awful feeling of grief. "I love you, Gramps. I hope there is a heaven. I really do."

With that, I stand up and take a few moments to harness my emotions and push them somewhere else, anywhere else that will allow me to stop crying. I wipe my tears, blow my nose, and take a deep breath before turning around and getting in the car with Uncle Charlie.

"You OK?" he asks.

"I'm fine," I reply coldly.

He turns onto the highway and heads back towards town for the reception, which I am dreading.

"Cruel man, God," Uncle Charlie says. "First he gives Dad Alzheimer's, then he takes his life before you can come home, before he can even process what has happened to him."

I want to smash Uncle Charlie's head through the windshield. My hatred startles me. I feel like the enraged bull I watched in Sevilla.

"You don't believe in God," I say sharply, trying to pick a fight.

"I do, too," he replies. "I pray, Atlas. I pray for you. I prayed for Dad. I pray."

"Oh, fuck you, Uncle Charlie!" I yell. He stares at me wide-eyed. "You *prayed* for Gramps? Maybe you should have gotten over yourself and visited him once in awhile. That would have been a miracle here on Earth. And if you really believed in God, in heaven, why is it cruel for him to take Gramps, huh? How would it be cruel for God to take Gramps to a better place? Don't you think God knows what is best for Gramps? You certainly don't." My face is warm and I am shaking with rage.

Uncle Charlie is silent for a while as we make a few turns, then finally pull into the parking lot of the church, where the reception will be held. Gramps used to come here a lot, when Grammy was alive, but he stopped going to church after she died.

Uncle Charlie parks, turns off the car, and faces me. "Well at least I was here when he died. During the worst of it, during the diagnosis. While you were off chasing a girl. It got hard and you bolted. You got out of here as fast as you could. Your ridiculous selfishness is something you need to think long and hard about, Atlas. You *really* think he didn't want you here? You *really* think that is what was best for him?"

I am too enraged to speak. His words are like bullets.

"No, you did what was best for *you*. You put yourself in front of him. You chose travel over family. You are just like all the people your age nowadays. It's all about me, me, me, me," he says pushing his index finger into my chest on the last "me." "It's all about you, Atlas. Who paid for the medical bills? Me and my boring job did. The job you are, somehow, too good for. The job that is below Prince Atlas and his high moral standards. Who sat with him in the hospital? I did!" He lets out a startling scream. His perfectly combed hair jolts out of place, and he takes a second to calm himself. He runs his right palm backwards from his forehead, over the hair, and looks in the rearview mirror.

"That's your job!" I scream back. "You are his kid! I'm his grandson. So don't act like you deserve a damn medal or something. I spent a lifetime with Gramps. He was my best friend. Can you say that? You squandered any chance at a relationship and now he is gone. You have to deal with that guilt now. Don't you?"

He smiles and waves out the car window as an old couple, dressed in black, makes their way past the car, into the church. I recognize them, but I don't wave.

"Gramps wanted me to be happy. That is why he bought me a ticket to Spain. He sent me. *He* wanted me to go."

"He wanted to be rid of you for a while for sure. It must have grown tiring for Dad, taking care of a grown man. All of your bitching," he scrunches up his nose and face, doing his best imitation of me and he speaks in a lowered, idiotic voice. "I just want to open a coffee shop. I want to fall in love. I need to find my path. I'm so sad. I'm so lonely. What is my purpose?"

His words are hitting their marks. They slice directly at my core, my doubts, my insecurities, and he has managed to make me feel foolish, which is his goal. I wish Gramps were here to defend me.

"Let this be a wake-up call, Atlas. Please. You are more lost than any person I know. Your parents wouldn't have wanted this. Gramps wouldn't have wanted this. It's time you grow up and stop chasing ridiculous fantasies and dreams," he says, more calmly this time.

Hot tears stream down my cheeks. I can't defend myself. I try, but the words are stuck; they catch in my throat. He puts his hand on my shoulder, and I manage to say, "Don't touch me." I pull away and stare out the window.

"Look. Next week, when you get over this little tantrum, we can talk about your future with my company. I will have to pull some strings to get you rehired but I would do that for you. We are all the family we have left, Atlas, like it or not," he says. The windows have steamed up with all of our anger.

He unbuckles his seatbelt and opens the car door. He gets out of the car and I follow. I feel an arm on my shoulder. It's my coworker, Amanda. She wasn't at the cemetery earlier, and I am surprised to see her. I haven't seen her since I left for Spain. It's good to see a familiar and friendly face.

"I'm so sorry, Atlas," she whispers while giving me a big hug. "I was late. The drive from Denver took longer than I thought it would. I'm so sorry. I know how much you loved your Gramps."

I don't speak for fear of losing hold of a hurricane of emotions running through me. I just purse my lips and offer a weak smile.

The reception is held in the church basement. Church volunteers have made a big pot of coffee and have set up some long wooden tables lined with beige metal folding chairs. Everything passes in a blur. I am a performer. I try to say the right thing to the right people. Sarah has come; she is out of her police uniform so I didn't recognize her at the cemetery. Uncle Charlie's wife didn't come since apparently their kid's soccer game was more important. They sent a card, though, with condolences scribbled on the back of a postcard-worthy family photo. The card is signed.

Dear Atlas,
Our deepest condolences. Your poor Uncle Charlie is a mess.
We are so sorry we couldn't be there. Our little soccer champion

has a big game this weekend but we hope you enjoy the flowers.
Sending you a big hug from Texas. Come down and visit us
sometime.
   With love,
   Your Aunt Nancy, Mark and Tim

The note accompanies an absurdly large floral arrangement,
which sits at the end of the table that is full of food. A large glass
vase holds white carnations, white snapdragons, and large white
lilies. Gramps hated floral arrangements.

I meet a few of Gramps's old friends. One couple used to play
cards with Gramps and Grammy, and they tell me they remember
me from when I was half as tall. Another man tells me that
Gramps made most of the furniture in his home. He tells me
Gramps was a good man and that he would have loved my
playing the trumpet at the funeral. I thank them all for coming,
one by one, and after everyone has finished eating sandwiches and
drinking coffee, Uncle Charlie gives a short speech.

He thanks everyone for coming, says his dad will be greatly
missed, and with that the church volunteers start to clean up.
Everyone slowly makes their way out of the church and into their
cold cars.

The day has faded to dark, and snow has begun to fall.
Snowflakes float through the glow of a street light above, slowly
drifting down to the pavement where it melts immediately. I hug
Sarah and Amanda and thank them again for coming.

Uncle Charlie and I get into the car, and we don't say a word
to each other. The 20-minute drive to the cabin seems to be taking
an eternity. We are both pulsing with hatred and blame. We focus
on anger to avoid pain.

He pulls up to the cabin and leaves the car running as I open
the door. "I'm going to get a hotel for the night, then head back to
Texas," he says.

"OK. Have a good one. Oh, and tell Aunt Nancy thanks for

the lovely flowers."

"Yep," he says.

I shut the door and watch him drive away. The red tail lights on his rental car slowly fade into the falling snow. He is gone, and I am alone.

CHAPTER TWENTY-ONE

Four calls of a crow outside in a pine tree wake me. The noise is unusually clear against the background of silence. I force myself to get out of bed and my feet hit the cold cabin floor. I can see my breath.

I head downstairs and look out of the large window by the wooden dining room table, where Gramps told me he had purchased my flight to Spain. Outside, the landscape is a perfect white. A blanket of snow sparkles in the morning sun, causing me to squint.

The cabin seems empty. I decide to brew some coffee, and the smell that fills the cabin reminds me of Gramps. Opting for ease, I turn on the electric space heater instead of starting a fire.

The black crow that woke me is perched in a tall pine tree down by the nearest crumbling cabin. It calls out repeatedly, and I watch it as I sip coffee in silence. Nothing answers its call, but the crow doesn't seem to mind.

Three weeks have passed since Gramps's funeral. I have spoken to no one, and a series of Colorado snowstorms and relentless cold have kept me here. I have survived on pancake mix, canned soup, and illegally caught rainbow trout that I obtained, with pleasure, from our neighbor's river. Luckily, Gramps always stocked up with supplies in bulk to limit his trips into town, so I have been just fine.

Loneliness is more real to me now than it has ever been. It seems as real as the crow perched in the tree outside, but bigger. The feeling overtakes me, amplifying itself with every passing day, causing me to have irrational thoughts. I spent all day yesterday convinced that even the deer that drink from the stream next to the cabin dislike me. This caused me to make a list of reasons I am alone and ways I might make a friend. I feel at the same time unloved and insignificant. I resent my circumstances and my lack of friends.

It's hardest in the evenings. When the day fades and the sky lights up with dazzling colors, I ache for someone to share it with. I want someone, anyone, to say trivial things to, like *Look at that sunset* or *What are we having for dinner?* But there is no *we*.

I have spent my days chopping wood, snowshoeing to the river to fish and trying to figure out my next move. I have plowed the road to the cabin each morning with the rusty truck, trying to keep my mind busy. Every day that passes, the loneliness I feel seems to grow deeper, like the snow outside.

My only companions are the woodchucks, deer, elk, crows, and the mountains that I can always count on like dependable friends. The mountain peaks watch me go about my day-to-day activities, never judging, always there, a force of good that somehow makes me feel better.

When the sun goes down and the stars appear in the cold night, I head inside to light a fire and heat up a can of soup, which I pair with saltine crackers and whisky. This is my new routine.

I have caught my reflection a few times in the window. I look older, weary and tired. The joy seems to be gone from my face and eyes. Not even I would want to be friends with my reflection. I have let my beard grow wild and showered only three times since I got here.

Apart from an e-mail from Pilar in Spain, asking me again if I found Isabel, and an e-mail from Uncle Charlie about Gramps's will, I haven't had any contact at all from the outside world. Several times I have uttered words for the simple purpose of checking to see if my voice still works.

The crow captures my attention again, skillfully hopping from branch to branch of the tree, pecking at the bark. It spots the carcass of a woodchuck, most likely killed by a coyote, and swoops down to pick at the frozen bones with its beak. Suddenly the bird is startled and flies away.

A police cruiser appears and slowly makes its way towards the cabin on the freshly plowed road. As it gets closer, I see Officer Piedmont inside. She parks, gets out of the cruiser, and grabs a cardboard box from the back seat, and carries it with her to the front door. Before she can knock, I open the door, greet her and invite her inside.

"Hi, Atlas," she says. "How are you doing?"

"Oh, you know. I'm OK," I reply.

"The hospital told me you never came to pick up your grandfather's things, so I hope you don't mind. I went and got them for you. They were going to throw everything away, and I thought you would want his things."

"Thank you. I, I completely forgot about that," I reply shaking my head. "Just set them here on the table. Can I get you anything? Coffee?"

I suddenly want her to stay. I have gotten used to the loneliness out here, but having contact with another human feels good. I am desperate for her to talk to me and spend some time, just a little time, distracting me from myself.

"I can't," she says. "I'm sorry. I'm on my morning break so I have to get back to town. Are you sure you are going to be OK?"

I try to fake a smile to make her feel better. "I'm fine. Don't worry about me. Really. Thanks for bringing this stuff out here."

"Of course. Look, Atlas. I know things are tough right now. But they always get better. I promise. They always get better. You have a future. A bright future. It's just not clear right now. It will be. Just because you can't see it, doesn't mean it's not there. Don't lose hope," she says. I just nod. "You take care, Atlas," she says and awkwardly shakes my hand. I cling to it, craving the touch of another human being. She pulls it away, and then makes her way back to the cruiser.

I stare into the flames of the fire and at the cardboard box filled with Gramps's things. I decide to rummage through his belongings, although I am not expecting to find much. Gramps was never one to collect things.

I pull out his red flannel shirt, which is folded neatly on top. I smell it and pain floods over me. It smells like coffee, sawdust, ChapStick, and pine. No one else in the world smells like him. I look back in the box to find his hospital wristband and his jeans, which I pull out of the box to place next to his flannel shirt. In the bottom of the box I spot an envelope, with my name on it. I grab it and examine every inch. The handwriting is Gramps's. I would recognize his chicken scratches anywhere.

I take a large gulp of whisky before opening the envelope. My throat burns. It's a one-page letter, written to me. I read each word carefully, afraid they will leap off the paper and escape into the night before I can grasp them.

Hey Tiger,
I just spoke with you on the phone. I know what is happening to me, and before I completely lose my marbles, I wanted to write you something while I am clear.

The fire pops, shooting a hot ember out onto the floor. I quickly scoop it up with the fire shovel and return it to the fire.

Life is a funny thing. Seeing your own child die is probably worse than Alzheimer's. At least with this disease I know I will probably soon forget I even had a daughter, or at least that she is dead.

I always felt responsible for you and your happiness. I shouldn't have let your parents go camping without at least a gun or something to protect them from the mad people of this world. After that awful thing that happened, I made it my mission to make sure you never suffered again. I wouldn't fail twice.

So that is my wish for you, Tiger. I want you to find your way. Remember the compass you got your mom for that camping trip? I don't know if you remember how they reacted to it, but they loved that thing. Remember where you were and how you were born, your name and that compass and find your way. You have the right instincts I know. You have iron boogers! We all do, but unfortunately, we let others be our compass, which is never a good idea.

I was happy in my life, and insane for being so. Life can be two things and it is your job to figure out which kind of life you want to live. I lived my life like someone floating in a canoe, downstream in a river, while everyone else was paddling upstream like madmen. I probably already told you this but I don't want you to forget.

Oars are an illusion, Tiger. Oars are an illusion. Do me a favor and follow your own inner compass, and you will float downstream in the direction you were born to go. Follow your curiosities, and when it feels like you are paddling too hard, remember to reset your course, to where it feels like you are floating effortlessly, blissfully downstream again.

I am glad you are not here to see me like this. It would be too much for you. You don't deserve it. I guess that is why I wanted to get you the hell out of here as soon as possible to go find that girl.

Well, I'm beat. My life was full because of you. I will die a poor man. For this I congratulate myself. This is probably the corniest thing you have ever read. From me anyway. But before my mind leaves me a shell of who I am, I just wanted to tell you, well Tiger, I love you, and dammit, if you stop pissing off our neighbor by fishing on his land, I will haunt you when I am gone.

Gramps

I laugh through my tears at his final line and smile. I feel the guilt suddenly lift and for the first time in weeks, I feel a little better. Maybe there is hope after all.

CHAPTER TWENTY-TWO

I spent a week in Denver following Gramps's advice. He left me the cabin in his will, so I have decided to stay in the cabin for a while before deciding what to do next. He also left me all of his money, which somehow worked out to be a negative number. I need to figure out how to pay the rest of his debts.

I broke the lease with my landlord in Denver, which was easily taken care of since Gwen has chosen to rent it from him long-term. I am lucky to have dodged the usual financial penalties, and I even got my deposit back, which provided me with some much-needed cash.

I have managed to sell the rest of my furniture on Craigslist and gift a few blankets and clothes to Gary, who is still living on the stoop of the apartment. Gary has changed, though, for the better, and I am thankful for some time to spend with him, before I say goodbye. We sit outside on the stairs. Gary is bundled up in a large blue parka to fight the cold of winter.

"How was your trip?" he asks. "Did you find the girl?"

"I didn't," I say. I shake my head and kick a rock from the step. It bounces around on the sidewalk, before hitting Gary's tin can.

"Well that sucks," he states simply. "Guess you better get a half dozen cats or a dog or somethin'."

"Very funny. What about you?" I ask. "Any big changes? How are they treating you down at the shelter?"

"I actually started going to AA," he replies, his head down. He isn't as happy-go-lucky as he usually is. He picks at a small hole in the leg of his snow pants. Maybe it's because he isn't drunk, but I find it hard to recognize him. I don't think I have ever met sober Gary, the real Gary.

"That's great, man. I'm really happy for you. Really I am," I say.

"You got me thinking, before you left," he says. "I guess I might have somethin' to do with this, with where I am. At least that is what they keep harpin' on in AA. *God grant me the serenity to accept the things I cannot change, and the wisdom to know the difference.* They say that all the damn time. I feel like a damn monk with all the chanting we all do together. There are some real emotional guys in there. It ain't easy though. I fuckin' hate bein' sober. I hate it, Atlas. Reality is a real painful bitch of a pill to swallow."

"Do you *really* though? Hate being sober?" I ask.

"I don't know. I guess we will see what happens," he says. "I don't get headaches every mornin' so I guess that's somethin'. I haven't puked in a few weeks either, and I'm gaining weight."

"Hey, at least you had the courage to try something different. What you were doing wasn't working, so good for you, giving it a try," I say. "If we don't try, things will never change."

He looks up at me and grins. His eyes aren't wild anymore. The pain is on the surface now, not buried inside, beneath the booze. "I could say the same thing to you."

"Yep, I guess you could, I guess you could," I reply. With that, I put a one hundred-dollar bill in his tin can and walk away. He doesn't say 'I love you, Atlas', as he used to, he is not drunk enough for that, but I can feel the respect between us both. I hope his quest ends better than mine has.

I stop by the coffee shop before heading back to Gunnison and give them the news that I will not be returning, which for them was not a surprise. Amanda wasn't there, so I tell them all to say goodbye to her as well. I then pack up the truck and head back to Gunnison.

As I make the familiar drive, climbing over Monarch Pass and crossing the Continental Divide, I am filled with hope.

For what, I don't yet know, but at the very least, the letter from Gramps has allowed the thick fog of sadness to begin to clear. I have made a clean break from my life in Denver, and now I just have to figure out where to go from here.

The truck only gets about 10 miles per gallon, so I stop yet again for gas in Gunnison to fill up before heading out to the cabin.

It's a cold afternoon, and I can feel snow threatening. I am thankful I got over the mountains before the storm hits. I pop the hood and refill the windshield wiper fluid. I then head inside for a snack and to pay in cash. The same woman who always seems to be working here recognizes me. Last time I snapped at her for trying to sell me a pumpkin spiced coffee. Her brows draw down in a scowl. I smile and surprise myself before heading out of town. Smiling is not my usual reaction.

The old truck only has an AM radio. Gramps was too cheap to pony up for a new AM/FM radio so I scan the limited channels, finally landing on a station that is playing classic big band tunes that I know Gramps would have loved.

As I turn onto the dirt road leading to the cabin, I notice fresh tire tracks in the snow heading up past Joe Peanut's grave, which is odd. Especially since I haven't been here for a full week. I proceed cautiously past the grave, past the crumbling old school house, and spot a white car parked in front of the cabin. I don't recognize the car and hope it isn't Uncle Charlie. The hair stands up on the back of my neck, and I don't know why. My spirit seems to sense something I can't quite see. Electricity replaces the blood in my veins.

Snow starts to slowly fall, as I predicted, and as I open the truck door I notice white exhaust coming from the tail pipe of the parked mystery car.

Who would be visiting me up here? I approach the car slowly, from behind. My mind quickly goes through a possible checklist of who it might be. *Officer Piedmont? Uncle Charlie? A lawyer? Our neighbor Jim? Amanda?*

Two big brown eyes study me in the rearview mirror, and the front car door swings open. A girl steps out of the car, and my jaw drops as her face turns towards mine. It's Isabel. *But how?*

She smiles, raises her arm and waves quietly with her fingers. I am frozen, stuck to the snow on the ground. Her brown hair, eyes, and face are exactly as I remember.

She looks down, fussing with black gloves and the zipper on her green coat. The snow is falling harder now, her hair full of snowflakes. Her cheeks are wet from melting snow and red with cold.

All I can do is stare. Something I have searched for, longed for, traveled for and lost, has found *me*. I am stunned, but gather my senses and turn off the truck before approaching her through the falling snow. This doesn't make sense. This can't be real.

We don't speak for what seems like an eternity, until she breaks the silence. "Hola, Atlas. I don't know if you remember me but—"

"Isabel," I interrupt her. She smiles, and the electricity I felt when I first met her resonates through me. My knees feel weak. I want to hug her, but we don't even know each other, so I refrain. It is as if we are two large magnets, and it is all I can do to keep my distance. I could almost touch the supernatural pull between us.

"What are you doing here?" I ask.

"Looking for you of course," she replies and blows warm air into her hands. "It's so cold in Colorado."

"You must be freezing. Would you like to come inside?" I ask.

"*Si, si.* Let me turn off the car," she says, smiling again.

My hands are shaking as I fumble for the keys and try to unlock the cabin door. A piece of paper is folded and wedged into a crack next to the doorknob. The note is written, unmistakably, in her beautiful handwriting, which I studied for so long in the guidebook.

Atlas,
I don't know if you remember me, but you never called. I am staying at the Redwood Inn, in town. I will be here for a few days.
Isabel (The Spanish girl from the coffee shop)

I manage to unlock the door and quickly tidy up the cabin, which is embarrassingly dirty. I cover a pile of dirty dishes with a tea towel, and scan the room for anything else that will embarrass me. I throw a banana peel and an open soup can quickly into a plastic bag and hide it in the kitchen.

Before I can tidy up anymore, she opens the door and walks inside. I watch her face, which is more beautiful than I remember. She looks around the cabin, then again over at me.

"Um. Would you like a coffee or tea?" I ask.

"Yes. You are the barista," she says. "A coffee would be nice. You told me when we first met that you are especially good at making coffee."

I am glad of the task, something to make me move instead of standing in the middle of the room like an idiot. I get to work in the kitchen and watch her out of the corner of my eye. She rubs her hands together, and she blows on them again.

"Do you have heat?" she asks.

"Ahh. Yes, sorry. Let me start a fire," I say, but she beats me to it.

"You make the coffee, and I will start the fire. My parents have a fireplace in Spain."

She stacks the small twigs and kindling in the fireplace and builds a teepee over crumpled newspaper before striking a long match, lighting the paper, and watching the fire grow.

I grab my special roast. The expensive stuff I now only allow myself to drink on Sundays because I am broke. But for her, for her, I will make the good stuff. If this were the last cup of coffee I drank on Earth, it would be worth it. Her very presence fills me with a type of joy I have not felt for a very long time.

She has made her way to the wall next to the fire, which is lined with photos of me, Gramps, Mom, and even Uncle Charlie. The framed photos are lit by firelight.

"Is this you as a kid?" she asks.

"Yep, that's me. I was about nine, I guess, in that one. And that picture is of my Gramps."

In the picture, my grin is full of missing teeth, as I proudly hold up a line of rainbow trout in front of the cabin. I am dressed in a Hawaiian shirt and a fisherman's hat. Gramps stands next to me, his arm around my shoulder.

"Soooo cute," she jokes and brushes my arm with her hand.

As I stand next to her, showing her the photos and waiting for the coffee to brew, I can smell her perfume. The intoxicating fragrance hints of Granada—a wonderful bouquet of almond blossoms, lemon trees, spices, and pine.

"Have a seat," I say. I am embarrassed by the empty glasses on the floor next to the chairs by the fire and a half-empty bottle of Colorado whisky. They are surrounded by used tissues, which I have been sniffling into, drunk weeping at night. I grab the glasses, tissues and whisky, carrying them to the kitchen sink.

"It looks like you had a sad party." She is flirting with me, but I am mortified. I simply shrug my shoulders and smile awkwardly.

We both take a seat in the two armchairs in front of the fire. She looks so foreign sitting there, in Gramps's place by the fire. She takes a sip of coffee, cupping the warm mug with her hands, as I stare at her like a fool.

"It is good coffee, mister barista," she smiles again.

She has a few freckles on her cheeks, which I study as she removes her coat. I notice four or five bracelets on her left wrist and a small tattoo of an olive branch on her ankle.

"So, you are probably wondering how I got here," she begins. I have no idea what she knows and simply nod my head. I wish to God that I could read her thoughts. Something catches her attention, and a big smile spreads across her face. I follow her gaze and am horrified by what she has spotted.

"Is that my guidebook?" she gets up and grabs it, fanning through the pages, the yellow sticky notes and all. I am beyond embarrassed and allow myself a defeated sigh. "Yep, it sure is. It looks like you found my heart, Atlas Green. AG."

I try to think of an explanation that won't make me sound insane. I get up to put another log on the fire.

"I lost your number, and I, I would have returned it, but, well ... my Gramps actually found the AG with the heart, not that I told him to investigate or anything, I just—"

She interrupts me. "I know you were in Spain, Atlas. It's OK. It's beyond sweet," she says. She looks me directly in the eyes, and I fight the urge to kiss her.

"You met my aunt in Granada. She told me a nice boy came looking for me. A boy who didn't speak any Spanish, but she could tell you were on a romantic mission. She said the dog liked you, so you couldn't be all that bad," she says.

The fire is roaring now, and I can feel the heat filling the room and warming my face. It's a full-on blizzard outside. Snowflakes swirl outside the window in the light from the cabin, like schools of tiny white fish in a dark expanse tightly rolling together as they disappear into the unknown.

"But how did you know I was here?" I ask.

"You told my aunt your name," she states the obvious. "And I remembered you from the coffee shop. I was quite mad at you for not calling me, you know. I thought you just didn't like me. You made me sad."

"I would have, but I lost your number that night," I explain.

"I know, well, I know *now* anyway. And you used my guidebook to track me down?"

"I tried to track you down," I say. We both take long sips of our coffee. "Why didn't you eat at *Los Diamantes*? I was there waiting on my last night in Granada because your aunt told me you were probably going to eat there," I say.

"I didn't know you were there. I didn't learn that you were looking for me until about a week after you knocked on her door. I think I was probably eating dinner at a friend's flat that night."

"I also went looking for you at the *Mirador de San Nicolas*. The art guy from the apartment ... "

"Ahh yes, I remember him. He was pretty crazy," she says and laughs.

"He told me you were going to watch the sunset so I staked out the plaza hoping to see you," I say.

"It sounds like we just barely missed each other. I watched the sunset a couple of times but not on the same day as you I guess. But I'm here now," she says.

The fire cracks and pops. The firelight dances on the wooden walls of the cabin around us, at the same time projecting shadows of indistinct objects.

"Atlas, that is possibly the most romantic thing anyone has ever attempted for me." She leans across the side table and places her hand softly on my knee. Her touch sends magical energy through my body. The feeling startles me. I have never felt such a draw, such a connection with someone. I am at the same time relieved that she wasn't something my mind invented, like a rose-colored memory exaggerated by time.

"I'm glad you think so," I reply and smile. "You know, I thought if I was able to find you, that you might think I was some crazy stalker. But now, you show up here at the cabin. How did you find me?"

"I went back to the coffee shop, and instead of you, I found

Amanda. She was very helpful and excited. She gave me your address, and she told me your Gramps had just died, and that I could find you here," she explains.

I mentally make a note to thank Amanda for delivering Isabel to my door.

"But why would you come all the way here for me?" I ask. She smiles and thinks for a minute before replying.

"Why did you come all the way to Spain to find me? My mom used to tell me, you will never believe in love at first sight, unless it happens to you. I don't know if I will love you someday, Atlas, but we met and you came to Spain looking for me, and well, I had to see. I had to ..."

"Follow your curiosity?"

"Exactly," she says.

I want to jump around the room. She feels the same way as I do. This is confirmation that I am not crazy.

"I remember at Speedy Coffee you told me you wanted to open your own shop someday. You should open your coffee shop, Atlas. Maybe in Granada," she says. I interpret this as only half joking. "What would you call your shop? Have you thought about a name at all?"

"Not really. I don't know what I would call it. I haven't thought about it I guess. You name it, and I will come to Granada," I reply.

"OK. Challenge accepted, Atlas Green. How about? Hmmmm. What did your grandfather call you again? Kitty?" She laughs and lightly touches my hand with hers.

"Tiger," I say.

"How about Tiger Coffee?" she says.

"Wow. That's good. I mean really good."

"I know it is. I guess you will have to move to Granada. You better start learning some Spanish, though," she says teasing me.

"I speak Spanish. Listen. *Dos cafés con leche por favor*," I say as she giggles.

"You have some work to do. But don't worry I will teach you," she says. Our eyes lock. She strokes the top of my hand with her fingers. It feels like we are making plans, together, but I can't be sure if she is serious.

"I have to know. Why did you buy an English guidebook about Spain, in Colorado?"

"I decided while I was traveling that I needed to move. I was living in Northern Spain, and I was unhappy there. So when I was in the bookstore I saw the book with the maps in it and decided to start apartment hunting before I changed my mind. They didn't have any Spanish versions," she explains.

"Where did you finally end up living? Where is your apartment?" I ask.

"I actually decided to rent a room from my aunt for a while," she says. "Her cave house is very cozy, and I get my exercise built into my day. You remember, I am sure, how high up she lives on that hill."

We switch to whisky and stay up all night talking. Hours pass in a dizzying blur. I tell her about my parents, the broken compass, and we pry into each other's dreams. We talk about life, Gramps, my Spanish adventure, and I ask her everything, wanting to know it all, what makes her *her*.

I learn she loves music, plays the guitar just for fun, loves french fries and chocolate and is probably the only person from Spain who likes baseball. She has a new job in Granada, working as a waitress in a fancy restaurant in the *Albayzín*. Her dream is to open a *panadería,* a bakery, and sell sweets and cakes, and yes, she loves coffee. She has two brothers, her parents are divorced, and well, I met her aunt.

Finally, the sun comes up, and the storm is gone. The first rays of the sun light up the cabin and make the fresh snow sparkle like a field full of diamonds.

"I guess we better get some sleep," I laugh, rubbing my tired eyes.

"I guess so," she says. "Atlas, I am so glad I came here. To meet you. I was so nervous. You wouldn't believe how nervous I was knocking on the cabin door. I was so afraid you might answer. I was also afraid you wouldn't."

"Me too," I reply. "And believe me, I know exactly how nervous you felt knocking on that door."

I make up her bed downstairs in Gramps's old room and ensure she has what she needs before heading upstairs. She catches me before I head up and grabs my hand. I don't know if it is possible to feel more happiness. I don't think it could fit inside of my body. She stands on her toes and kisses me lightly on the cheek, holding her lips against my skin for a few glorious seconds.

"Sleep well. I will see you in a few hours," she says with a smile. With that, she heads into Gramps's bedroom, and I make my way upstairs. I cover the windows with pillowcases to block out the light of day and lie down, exhausted but every inch of me is content. She is amazing. She is everything I remember her to be. She is pure magic. *She* found *me*.

See, I told you so. I hear Gramps as if he were in the room. *I told you to follow your curiosity, Tiger. Good for you, boy. Good for you.*

I feel the presence of Gramps and my parents, as real as the magic I had forgotten, and begin to cry. A joyful cry this time. One of relief, that sometimes things actually do work out, even for a lost, wandering soul like me.

If it doesn't open, it's not your door. The words from the man with the heater in Granada pop into my head, causing me to smile. *How many people actually try any doors at all?* Gramps always told me "try harder" when I complained about love or life, which I never really understood, until now.

Maybe that's what my parents meant by encouraging me to be a seeker. Perhaps the whole point is to experiment with the doors of life and see where they lead you. A closed door is not a failure, it is a clue. If I have the courage to listen to those clues, then I will have learned to follow my own inner compass, which is constantly pulling me towards my own happiness. I simply made the choice, with some encouragement from Gramps, to try a few doors.

It feels good to believe in magic again. It feels right and true. A long held guilt about my parents' deaths slowly lifts, causing me to feel lighter somehow. I am glad I buried their broken compass with Gramps. They taught me how to use it, and now I feel like I can finally let it go. Not because I want to forget, but because I don't need it anymore.

It's time to find my own true north.

AUTHOR'S NOTE

This is a work of fiction. However, the ghost town of Baldwin, Colorado, does exist and is still filled with crumbling cabins to this day. New Baldwin does in fact date back to 1909, and I spent my childhood exploring this town, the old schoolhouse, and paying my respects at Joe Peanut's grave. I also spent many weekends fishing in Ohio Creek, with my Gramps.

ACKNOWLEDGMENTS

This book would not exist without a wonderful group of people that helped me along the way. Thank you to my manuscript readers. To Matt Rooney, for convincing me that art in all forms is exactly what the world needs now and always. To Jeremy René, a fellow writer, who spent hours reading through this body of work, offering his time and challenging me to find the true heart of this story with incredibly honest feedback.

Thank you to Bridget Verrette, a talented editor and friend whose patient guidance through multiple versions of this book were invaluable. Thank you to my copy editor, Agnes Bannigan, for her enthusiasm, professionalism, kindness, and attention to detail.

Finally, thanks to my best friend and wife, Amy, for encouraging me to bring this story to life over the past few years. Your positivity and feedback kept me writing when I faltered. And to Gramps, who took me fishing every summer.

More by Gabriel Schirm

SUNRISES TO SANTIAGO: SEARCHING FOR PURPOSE ON THE CAMINO DE SANTIAGO

A true-life account of a search for purpose and meaning along the historic 490-mile pilgrimage route called the Camino de Santiago in Spain.

"This book will leave you inspired to practice the same sense of adventure and to appreciate the smaller joys of life as a whole, whether you are gallivanting through Spain or picking up dog food at the grocery store"
–*The Dodge Voice*

PAZ
– PUBLISHING –

Questions For Discussion

Finding Tiger

———

1. It frequently takes courage to follow your path and take seemingly "crazy" chances. What courageous choices have you made in life that at the time seemed crazy but turned out to be wise?

2. Do you believe in magic? What is magic to you? Do you have a negative voice inside that discourages the natural or magical part of yourself? How does what you believe manifest itself in your life?

3. Who is the bull in this story? Who or what is the matador and his red cape? Did you notice the color red and its symbolism peppered throughout the book by the author? How was the color red used and why?

4. Atlas's relationship to his dead parents is complex, ranging from guilt to longing. What happens to a child when his or her parents are gone? Does this last well into adulthood as it does for Atlas?

5. Atlas keeps a "book of dreams" filled with the types of coffee he

would like to feature someday in his own coffee shop. What would fill your "book of dreams"?

6. Gramps encourages Atlas to follow his curiosity and try things that might make him nervous. What piques your curiosity?

7. Project into the future. Does Atlas open a coffee shop? Do Atlas and Isabel get married? Where do they live?

8. Do you feel Atlas was selfish for leaving Gramps alone to deal with Alzheimer's disease? Would you have made the same decision?

9. How would you describe Atlas and Isabel's relationship? What drew them together? Did you root for them to find each other?

10. What did you think of the compass and everything it represented for Atlas? Were you surprised when he left it in the ground with Gramps?

11. Who is the "Uncle Charlie" in your life? How does that person inform your decisions?

12. What was your childhood relationship with your grandfather like? Did you identify with Atlas's memories of being a young boy, fishing with Gramps?